Return to Del

Dread
Mountain

Maze
of the
Beast

The
Shifting
Sands

The Valley
the Lost

THE LAND O

The Shadowlands

The Lake
of Tears

City
of the
Rats

The Forests
of Silence

Del

DELTORA

N
W · E
S

VENTURE INTO DELTORA

Return to Del

EMILY RODDA

Scholastic Inc.
New York   Toronto   London   Auckland   Sydney
Mexico City   New Delhi   Hong Kong   Buenos Aires

ISBN 0-439-41951-4

12 11   7/0

Printed in the U.S.A.   40

First Scholastic club printing, April 2002

Contents

The story so far . . .

Lief, Barda, and Jasmine have found the seven lost gems of the magic Belt of Deltora. Now they must find the heir to Deltora's throne, for only when the Belt is worn by the true heir can the evil Shadow Lord be overthrown, and Deltora freed.

Lief's parents, now imprisoned in Del, told Lief that when they helped King Endon and Queen Sharn to escape the city on the coming of the Shadow Lord, over sixteen years ago, a hiding place was planned for the royal couple and their unborn child. But the companions have learned that this plan failed when the magical people of Tora broke their ancient vow of loyalty, and refused to offer refuge. The Torans were banished to the Valley of the Lost, and the royal family's whereabouts are unkown.

Doom, the grim, mysterious leader of the Resistance, left the companions in anger when they refused to heed his warning to keep away from the Valley of the Lost. Dain, a young Resistance fighter of about Lief's own age, reluctantly went with him. Now the valley has been freed of its evil enchantment, but Lief, Barda, and Jasmine do not know which way to turn. They must find the heir, but they do not know how. And the Shadow Lord's servants — Grey Guards, hideous shape-changing Ols, and huge vulture-like birds called Ak-Baba — are searching for them.

Now read on . . .

1 ~ Toran Magic

The Belt of Deltora was complete. Seven gems glowed once more in its gleaming medallions of steel. It was perfect. And yet . . .

Lief glanced at Barda and Jasmine, walking with him through the sunlit beauty of what had been the Valley of the Lost. In the blue sky above them, Kree sailed on the wind with others of his kind. Many birds had returned to the valley since the evil mist had lifted, the exiled people of Tora had been freed from their living death, and the evil Guardian had returned to his old character of the hermit Fardeep.

The three companions had triumphed. But now they had to face the fact that unless they found the heir to Deltora's throne all their efforts would have been in vain. They had believed that the Belt would lead them to the heir. But so far there had been no sign.

Sighing, Lief flipped open the little blue book he carried. This copy of *The Belt of Deltora* was one of the few things that had survived the destruction of the Guardian's palace. And why? Lief thought. Why, unless it holds the key? He stared again at the words he had read so often.

✝ **Each gem has its own magic, but together the seven make a spell that is far more powerful than the sum of its parts. Only the Belt of Deltora, complete as it was first fashioned by Adin and worn by Adin's true heir, has the power to defeat the Enemy.**

"Reading the words again will not change them, Lief," muttered Jasmine. "We must find the heir — and soon!" She plucked a berry and gave it to Filli. Many little furred creatures now thronged the valley. But all were larger than little Filli, who stayed shyly on Jasmine's shoulder, peering around with wondering eyes.

"If only we knew where to look!" Barda moved restlessly. "We cannot remain here any longer, waiting for a sign. At any moment — " He looked up, and his brow creased in a sudden frown. Lief, too, looked up, and was startled to see that where only moments before there had been clear blue, a swirling mist was gathering. The birds were wheeling, screeching . . .

Sharply, Jasmine called Kree, who broke away from the flock and came hurtling down towards her. At the same moment, Lief saw Fardeep approaching. Two Torans were with him: Peel, a tall, bearded man, and Zeean, a straight-backed old woman in a scarlet robe.

"Do not fear!" Fardeep called. "The Torans are weaving a veil of cloud to shroud the valley once more. The Shadow Lord must not discover that we are free."

"But what of the creatures?" Jasmine exclaimed.

"Our mist will not harm them, little one," smiled Zeean. "It is soft and sweet. Now that our magic has returned, we can do many things."

"Except the thing we want most," Peel said soberly. "Except return to Tora."

"Indeed." Zeean's eyes turned to Lief, Barda, and Jasmine. "And yet," she murmured. "I have hopes . . ."

Lief glanced quickly at Fardeep.

"Fardeep has said nothing, Lief," Zeean said. "But we remember what we saw just before the valley changed. You are carrying a precious thing — a thing that could save us all. Yet you are troubled. We can feel it. Can we not help?"

Lief hesitated. The habit of secrecy was strong. But perhaps, indeed, the Torans could help. Barda and Jasmine stirred beside him and he knew that they, too, felt the impulse to trust.

"Be aware," Zeean said softly, "that to tell one Toran is to tell all. We have no secrets from one another. But this is our strength. Between us we have much knowledge, and our memories are long."

Lief touched the Belt, heavy under his shirt. But before he could say a word, Zeean and Peel stiffened. "Strangers are entering the valley!" Peel hissed. "Walking quickly, along the stream."

"Friends?" Fardeep asked urgently.

Zeean shook her head, puzzled. "We cannot tell. Shape-changers — Ols — we can usually sense. Others of evil will also. But these minds are closed to us."

The light dimmed as the mist thickened. Lief made a decision. "We will go to meet them," he said. "And, on our way, we will talk."

And so it was that, walking in the greenness of the valley floor, the companions told the secret they had kept for so long. It was strange to speak the words aloud. But Lief felt no fear as the Torans drank in the sight of the Belt.

"The amethyst," Zeean whispered, gently touching the purple gem. "The Toran stone, symbol of truth."

"The Toran stone?" exclaimed Jasmine. "What do you mean?"

"Why, the Torans were one of the seven tribes who gave their talismans to Adin when the Belt of Deltora was first made," Zeean said.

"No doubt that is why the amethyst was in the

Maze of the Beast, so near to Tora," Peel added. "Once taken from the Belt, the gem yearned to return to its first place. As far as it could, it bent to its will the Ak-Baba which carried it. Perhaps — "

Two people rounded a bend in the stream ahead. One gave a cry, and broke into a run. Startled, Lief saw it was Dain, and that the man with him was Doom.

"Dain!" Doom bellowed. Dain glanced behind him guiltily, and his flying feet stumbled and slowed.

"Why, this boy looks very like one of us," Zeean murmured. "His hair — his eyes . . ."

"Dain's mother is of Toran blood," Lief told her. "His parents were taken by the Grey Guards a year ago. Now he works with Doom, in the Resistance."

Both of the visitors were now standing quite still. Doom glanced at the cloud above his head.

"All is well, Doom," Fardeep called. "Your friends here are safe. The mist is only for our protection."

Warily, Doom moved closer. He searched Fardeep's face, and his own face darkened. "You!" he snarled, reaching for his sword.

"No!" Lief exclaimed. "Doom, this is Fardeep. He is no longer the Guardian. No enemy of ours, or of yours."

For the first time since Lief had known him, Doom looked baffled. "You have much to explain!" he muttered.

"As you do," said Barda harshly. "Why did you keep your knowledge of this place from us?"

"I warned you against the Valley of the Lost with all my strength!" Doom growled, recovering a little. "Would it have helped if I had told you I had visited it myself? No! You would have decided that if I could escape its dangers, so could you."

"Perhaps," snapped Jasmine. "But you take your wretched love of secrecy too far, Doom! Why did you not say that you believed the Guardian was King Endon?"

Ignoring Dain's gasp of horror, Doom smiled grimly. "Even *I* have some fine feelings. When I left this accursed valley I swore that never from my lips would my people learn what their king had become. They had suffered enough. Far better, I thought, to let them believe he was dead."

"You played into the Shadow Lord's hands, then," said Lief quietly. "He wants the king forgotten, so his own hold over Deltora can never be broken."

Doom flinched, as though he had received a blow. Slowly he rubbed his brow with the back of his hand, hiding his eyes. Dain was staring straight ahead, his face quite expressionless. But it seemed to Lief that behind the calm mask many different feelings were struggling.

After a long moment, Doom dropped his hand and looked straight at Lief, Barda, and Jasmine. "I believe I know why you came here," he said. "Am I to understand that you succeeded in your quest?"

The companions remained silent.

A shadow crossed Doom's face. "Perhaps you are wise not to trust me," he said bitterly. "Perhaps, in your place, I, too, would keep silence." He turned away. "Come, Dain," he said to the boy standing rigidly beside him. "We are not needed here. Or wanted, it seems."

Zeean stirred. "Wait!" she cried.

Doom swung around, unsmiling.

"We cannot afford suspicion and rivalry now," the woman said, standing very straight. "United, we drove the Shadow Lord and his abominable hordes from our lands in the time of Adin. United, we can do it now."

She turned to Lief, Barda, and Jasmine. "The time for secrecy between friends is past," she said firmly. "You are hunted, and you do not know what your next step should be. We need the talents and experience of all who share our cause. Now, at last, it is time to trust."

✳

They returned to the clearing beside Fardeep's hut. There, while bees hummed among the flowers and the sun sank in the sky, the story was told once more. When, at last, Lief showed the Belt, Dain gasped and shrank back, trembling. "I knew that you had some mighty aim," he whispered, "I knew it!"

But Lief was watching Doom. The man's face had not changed. What was he thinking?

"Some of what you have told us I had already guessed," Doom muttered at last. "No one who has travelled this land as I have done could have failed to hear the legend of the lost Belt of Deltora. I came to believe that you were seeking it — but whether for reasons of good or ill, I did not know."

His mouth tightened. "Now I regret my suspicion that you were working against our cause. But — " He ran his lean brown hands through his tangled hair. "Can it be true that this — this legend made real — can help Deltora? Perhaps, long ago, in the years that are dark to me, I would have accepted such a tale. But as it is — "

"You must believe!" Jasmine burst out. "The Shadow Lord himself fears the Belt. That is why the gems were taken and hidden in the first place!"

Doom regarded her thoughtfully. "How many gems does the Shadow Lord know you have?" he asked.

"We have strong hopes that he thinks we are still to reach Dread Mountain, the Maze of the Beast, and this valley," Lief answered.

"Hopes are no basis for planning," said Doom curtly.

Lief felt a prickle of irritation. He was not alone.

"We are as aware of that as you, Doom!" exclaimed Jasmine angrily. "No one would welcome certain knowledge more than we would!"

Looking from one to the other, Zeean sighed, and rose. "Let us rest, now," she said. "In the morning, our minds will be clearer."

As she and Peel quietly left the clearing, Doom shrugged and strode off to where his belongings lay. Dain hurried after him. Fardeep wandered back to his hut to begin preparing food.

"Doom is an uncomfortable ally," Barda muttered. "But he is right in wanting facts, rather than hope."

"Then we will give him facts!" Jasmine snapped. "Lief must use the last of the water from the Dreaming Spring."

Lief nodded slowly. They had been saving the water for when they really needed it, but surely that time had arrived. If he visited his imprisoned father again, the evil Fallow might come to the cell. Then Lief could learn how much the Shadow Lord knew. But what if Fallow did not come?

Lief's heart sank as he saw what must be done. He could not risk visiting his father or mother. Instead, he must use the magic water to spy on Fallow himself.

2 - Fallow

Much later, Lief lay still in the darkness. His eyelids were very heavy, but his mind was fighting sleep. He was afraid — afraid of what he would see. Who was Fallow? *What* was he? Lief thought he knew. Words he had heard Fallow say to his father echoed in his mind:

. . . where one dies, there is always another to take his place. The Master likes this face and form. He chose to repeat it in me . . .

Lief had not known what that meant, when first he heard it. Now he knew only too well.

Fallow was an Ol, and perhaps — almost certainly — one of the Grade 3 Ols Doom had heard of in the Shadowlands. The triumph of the Shadow Lord's evil art. An Ol so perfect, so controlled, that no one could tell it was not human. An Ol that could mimic nonliving things as well as living creatures. An Ol that was evil and powerful beyond anything Lief could imagine.

Prandine, King Endon's chief advisor, had been one such being. Of that Lief was sure. Fallow, made in his image, had taken up the Shadow Lord's work where Prandine had finished.

Lief turned restlessly. Queen Sharn had killed Prandine — tipped him from the palace tower window to crash to his death. Grade 3 Ols paid a price for their perfection, then. They could die as humans could.

He closed his eyes and forced his mind to go blank. It was time to give in to the Dreaming Water. Time to visit the world of Fallow.

✳

White walls, hard and gleaming. A gurgling, bubbling sound. And in the corner a tall, thin figure — Fallow — shuddering in a shower of sickly green light, bony arms flung high. His mouth was gaping open like the jaws of a skull, its corners thick with foam. His eyes had rolled back so only the whites showed, shining, horrible . . .

Lief choked back his cry of horror, though he knew he could not be heard. His stomach churned, but he could not look away.

Thump! Thump!

Lief jumped violently as the sound, like a great heartbeat, throbbed through the room.

The green light disappeared. Fallow's long arms dropped to his sides. His head fell forward.

Thump! Thump!

Lief clamped his hands over his ears. But still the sound vibrated through him, filling his mind, making his teeth chatter. It was unbearable. But it seemed to compel him. It seemed to be calling him. Wildly he searched the room, looking for its source.

Then he saw it. A small table in the center of the room. A table that looked like any other, except that its glass surface was thick and curved — and moving like water. Lief felt himself drawn forward. The urge to look into that moving surface, to answer the summons, was irresistible.

But, panting, Fallow was stumbling out of the corner, snatching a cloth from his sleeve. Wiping his face hurriedly he staggered towards the table and leaned over it, staring down at the rippling surface.

The throbbing sound lessened, dimmed. The ripples grew smoky, rimmed with red. And deep in the midst of the grey and red there was a hollow darkness.

Fallow leaned closer. A voice hissed from the darkness. Deathly quiet.

"Fallow."

"Yes, Master." Fallow quivered, his mouth still flecked with drying foam.

"Do you abuse my trust?"

"No, Master."

"You have been given the Lumin for your pleasure in your place of exile. But if you neglect your duties because of it, it will be removed."

Fallow's eyes darted to the corner where the green light had showered, then swerved back to the table surface. "I do not neglect my duties, Master," he whimpered.

"Then what news do you have for me? Has the blacksmith Jarred confessed at last?"

His heart wrung, Lief pressed his hands together in an agony of fear.

"No, Master," said Fallow. "I think — "

"Is someone with you, slave?" the voice hissed suddenly.

Startled, Fallow whirled around and scanned the room. His dull eyes passed over Lief, standing motionless behind him, without a flicker.

"No, Master," he whispered. "How could there be? As you ordered, no one enters this room but me."

"I felt . . . something." The darkness in the center of the whirling shadows grew larger, like the pupil of a giant eye widening.

Lief stood still as a stone, trying to keep his mind blank, holding his breath. The Shadow Lord could sense him. That evil mind was probing the room, trying to find him. He could feel its malice.

"There — there is no one here." How strange to see Fallow cowering, those cruel lips trembling.

"Very well. Continue."

"I — have begun to think the blacksmith indeed knows nothing," Fallow stammered. "Starvation and torment have not moved him. Even the threat of death or blindness for his wife did not cause him to speak."

"And she?"

"If anything, she is stronger than her husband. She rails at her tormentors, but says nothing of use."

Mother. Lief felt hot tears trickling down his cheeks. He did not dare move to wipe them away. He held himself rigidly, trying to cut off his mind from his heart.

"They have made a fool of you then, Fallow," whispered the voice from the darkness. "For they are guilty — guilty of everything we suspected. Their son is one of the three. There is no doubt."

Fallow gaped. "Their son is with the king? But the blacksmith laughed when I suggested it. Laughed! I could have sworn the laughter was real."

"It was. The man who is travelling with the boy is not Endon, but a palace guard named Barda. No doubt Jarred found your mistake amusing."

Fallow's face twisted with rage. "He will pay!" he croaked. "And the woman, too. They will wish they had never been born! I will — "

"You will do *nothing*!" The hiss was icy. Fallow grew rigidly still.

"Perhaps you have been living too long among human peasants, Fallow, and have started to think as they do. Or perhaps too much use of the Lumin has weakened the brain you were given by my hand."

"No, Master. No!"

"Then listen to me. You are my creation, whose only purpose is to do my will. Do exactly as I tell you. Keep the blacksmith and the woman safe. I have need of them. While they live, they can be used against the boy. Once they are dead, we have no hold over him."

"Beings in their shapes —"

"He wears the great topaz. The spirits of his wretched dead will appear to him, the moment they leave the world. Ols in their shapes will not deceive him."

There was silence. Then Fallow spoke again.

"May I ask where the three are now, Master?"

"We have lost sight of them. For now."

"But, I thought your —"

"Do not think of what does not concern you, Fallow! Curiosity is for humans, not for such as you. Is that understood?"

"Yes, Master. But I was not asking for myself — only out of concern for your plans. The three may, by some miracle, restore the Belt. And this will — displease you."

The words were humble. But Lief thought he saw a tiny spark of rebellion in the downcast eyes.

Perhaps the Shadow Lord saw it, too, for the swirling red that edged the grey seemed to flare, and a crafty note entered the hissing voice.

"I have many plans, Fallow. If one does not succeed, another will. If you follow my orders exactly, sooner or later you will be free to have what sport you wish with the boy's mother and father. And with Endon himself, if he at last lifts his cowering head and crawls out of hiding."

A chill ran down Lief's spine.

"And the three?" Fallow asked greedily.

There was a long, low laugh. The red swirls deepened to scarlet.

"Oh, no. The three, Fallow, will be mine."

❋

Lief awoke, his heart thumping, his stomach knotted. There was a sour taste in his mouth — the taste of fear and misery.

He was not sure how long he had been asleep. Moonlight still filtered palely through the Torans' cloud, flooding the clearing with its dim, mysterious glow. Lief forced himself to lie still until the pounding of his heart had quietened. Then, quietly, so as not to wake the other sleepers, he roused Barda and Jasmine.

With the ease born of long practice, they were instantly awake and alert, reaching for their weapons.

"No! There is no danger," Lief whispered. "I am sorry to disturb your rest. But I had to speak with you."

"You learned something!" hissed Jasmine, sitting up.

Lief nodded. He glanced over to where Doom and Dain lay, and, lowering his voice still further, told of what he had seen and heard. He made himself tell it all, biting his lip to stop his voice from shaking.

His companions listened in silence till the end.

"So he hopes that we will fall into his hands," Barda muttered. "We shall see about that!"

Lief glanced at him. The big man's fists were clenched and his face was filled with grief and anger.

Jasmine put her hand on Lief's arm. "At least we know that for now your parents are safe, Lief," she said softly. "And Doom can stop his sneering. We were right. The Shadow Lord is not certain where we are."

Barda nodded. "And, plainly, he does not know where Endon, Sharn, and their child are, either. He thinks that we will lead him to the heir's hiding place."

Lief's stomach was churning. "And perhaps we will," he breathed. "For do you not see what else we have learned?"

They both stared at him blankly. He swallowed and went on. "The Shadow Lord has found out who you really are, Barda. And he knows my name as well. How could that be? Unless . . ."

"Unless someone in the Resistance stronghold is a spy!" whispered Jasmine, suddenly realizing the truth. "For it was at the stronghold that Barda's name was revealed to all, by that acrobat, Jinks. And no doubt Dain told Lief's name, and mine, while we were imprisoned. He would not have seen the harm."

Lief gnawed at his lip. "And someone — someone in the stronghold has made contact with the Shadow Lord. Dain told us that Doom suspected there was a spy in the Resistance. This proves it."

"Glock!" hissed Jasmine with loathing.

"Or Jinks himself," Barda muttered. "It could be anyone."

"Yes," said Lief, glancing again at the sleeping figures of Dain and Doom. "It could be anyone at all."

3 - Suspicion

Noiselessly, the companions gathered their belongings and stole out of the clearing. In moments they were moving along the stream, towards the valley's end. They knew that it would be folly to try to escape by climbing. The cliff walls were too steep, too slippery with loose stones.

It was cold and dim under the trees. Everywhere Torans lay sleeping under the shelters they had made.

What will they think when they wake and find us gone? Lief thought. But he and his companions had no choice but to flee. Following Zeean's well-meaning advice, they had revealed their precious secret to two people whose friendship was now far from certain.

Lief bitterly regretted that he had not been more wary.

We cannot tell, Zeean had whispered, when Fardeep asked her if the visitors to the valley were friends or foes.

Why could the Torans not tell if Dain and Doom were of good or evil will? Surely only because one or both of them were skilled at veiling their minds. This could be habit — completely innocent. Or —

I have many plans . . .

The evil whisper swirled in Lief's mind like a foul mist.

He looked ahead, and realized that they were nearly at the end of the valley. The space between the rocky cliffs was closing. They were reaching the narrow pass through which Doom and Dain had come.

"There is something across the valley entrance," Jasmine breathed. "Something is blocking our way."

And indeed now Lief could see for himself a large shape lying across the stream. As he crept closer he saw that it was a caravan. On the driver's seat, rolled in a blanket, lay a man, gently snoring.

"Steven," breathed Barda. "He must have come with Dain and Doom. No doubt he is to follow them into the valley if they do not return within a certain time."

The caravan hulked before them. Its back doors were pressed close against one rocky cliff wall. They would have to pass it at the other end, right under Steven's nose. But he was still snoring gently under his blanket. Surely he would not wake!

They began moving forward. *One step, two . . .*

They were almost opposite the caravan now.

Three steps, four . . .

The snoring stopped. Lief looked over at the rolled bundle on the driver's seat. It was silent, and absolutely still. Too still.

Lief's heart seemed to freeze. Then, abruptly, there was a terrible growling sound, and the blanket began to heave, as though the body inside was swelling, doubling in size.

"Here!" A voice from the trees split the air. Lief whirled and saw Doom pounding towards them.

On the caravan seat, something snarled like a huge animal. Hot, heavy breathing grew louder, louder . . .

"Nevets, go back!" Doom shouted. "This is Doom! There is no danger!" Roughly he pushed Lief, Barda, and Jasmine back into the trees and stood in front of them.

"There is no danger!" he shouted again.

Slowly, the growling faded. And when Lief managed to focus his eyes on the caravan once more, the form under the blanket had shrunk back to a normal size. As he watched, it turned over as if settling once more to sleep.

Doom began hustling the companions back the way they had come. "What game do you think you are playing?" he hissed furiously. "Do you want to die? If I had not woken and found you gone —"

"How could we know you had set your pet monster to guard the valley?" Jasmine flashed back furiously.

"And are we not free to do as we please?" Lief was boiling with anger and shock.

Doom's eyes narrowed. Then he turned on his heel and began walking back down the stream.

"I suggest you stay in the valley for now," he called back over his shoulder. "Even I would not risk troubling Steven again for an hour or two. And Zeean and Peel are very anxious to see you. It seems they have something to tell you."

✳

By the time the companions reached the clearing once more, dawn was breaking. Zeean, Peel, Fardeep, and Dain were gathered around a small fire, sharing a breakfast of hot, flat cakes dripping with honey from Fardeep's hives. They looked up as the companions approached with Doom, but asked no questions.

Perhaps they know that they will get no answers, thought Lief, taking his place at the fire with Barda and Jasmine. He felt a mixture of emotions: resentment at having had to return; curiosity as to what the Torans had to say; frustration at the thought that whatever it was would be heard by Doom and Dain also. Yet Doom had saved them from Nevets. Did that not mean . . . ?

"It is good you have returned," Zeean said, pushing the plate of cakes towards the newcomers. "We have an idea to discuss with you."

She paused, her brow creasing as she saw Barda, Lief, and Jasmine glance at Doom and Dain.

Lief gripped the Belt around his waist. The calm of the amethyst, the strength of the diamond, flowed through him. And suddenly he knew what must be done. He and his companions must act as though they had no doubts about their allies. At all costs, the knowledge they had gained through his dream must be kept secret. This would be their strength.

He smiled at Zeean, and casually reached for a cake. The woman seemed to relax, and began speaking once more.

"Your father told you that the Belt would lead you to the heir, Lief. But your father knows only what he has read. And that is perhaps not all there is to know."

"What do you mean?" Lief asked, frowning. He took a bite of the cake. It was warm and sweet on his tongue.

"The book — *The Belt of Deltora* — is a work of history, not of advice," said Peel eagerly. "The writer could not foresee that one day the gems would be torn from the Belt, and would not know what should be done in such an event."

"The Belt is a thing of great mystery and magic," Zeean added. "The gems have been restored. But perhaps this is not enough."

There was a muffled sound from the edge of

the group. Dain was leaning forward, as though he wanted to speak.

"Dain?" said Zeean.

Dain blushed as he always did when attention was drawn to him. "I was thinking of — of the story of how the Belt was made," he stammered. "And of what happened after."

He fell silent, glancing nervously at the silent Doom.

"Yes?" urged Zeean encouragingly. Her eyes were sharp with interest. Lief's skin began to tingle. Somehow he knew that they were on the edge of something momentous.

He pulled out the copy of *The Belt of Deltora* and flipped through it. In moments he had found what he was looking for — the words that told of how the blacksmith Adin had persuaded each of the seven tribes to allow its gem to join the Belt.

† The tribes were at first suspicious and wary, but, one by one, desperate to save their land, they agreed. As each gem became part of the belt, its tribe grew stronger. But the people kept their strength secret, and bided their time.

† And when at last the Belt was complete, Adin fastened it around his waist and it flashed like the sun. Then all the tribes united behind him to form a great army, and together they drove the enemy from their land.

Slowly, he read the words from the book aloud.

"The victory depended not only on the Belt, but on the union of the seven tribes, and their loyalty to Adin," said Peel slowly, when the reading was finished. "Is that what you are thinking, Dain?"

Dain nodded. Doom regarded him curiously.

"Why, you are quite a scholar, Dain," he said mockingly. "How did a farmer's boy learn so much of the history of Deltora?"

Dain flinched, but would not be cowed. "My parents taught me," he said quietly. "They never lost hope that one day Deltora would be free. They said its story should not be forgotten."

Doom shrugged and turned away, but Lief thought he saw a flicker in the dark eyes. Was it anger? Regret? Or something else?

"Your parents were wise indeed, Dain," Zeean was saying. "Your mother had Toran blood, did she not? What was her name?"

Dain seemed to tremble. "Her name is Rhans," he said, so softly that Lief could hardly hear him. "*Is*, not *was*. Why do you speak as though she is dead?"

Zeean looked distressed. "I am sorry," she said. "I did not mean — "

"So the seven tribes united under Adin and the Belt," Barda growled. "Why is this important to us?"

"Who knows?" muttered Doom. He got to his feet and moved a little away from the group, turning his back. Dain looked desperately at Lief.

25

"You must have been helped on your journey, Lief," he said in a low voice. "Throughout Deltora you met people willing to defy the Shadow Lord. Surely they will help you again. Help you to . . ." He glanced at Doom, and again his voice seemed to fail him.

Lief took a deep breath. "I think Dain's idea is that the uniting of Deltora formed part of the Belt's magic," he said. "Dain thinks that we should bring the seven tribes together once more."

4 - The Seven Tribes

Jasmine was the first to break the silence. "But the seven tribes existed in ancient days — or so I was told," she said. "Surely they are long gone, now."

"No, they are not," said Zeean. "Certainly, many in Deltora would not know from which tribe they sprang. The Del tribe, whose gem was the topaz, has spread far and wide. Other tribes have done likewise."

"But some tribes have remained the same," Peel put in. "The Torans, for example. And the Dread Gnomes."

"The Dread Gnomes were one of the seven?" Lief's heart began to pound.

"Indeed," nodded Zeean. "The great emerald was the gnomes' talisman."

Lief shook his head in amazement. Fa-Glin and

Gla-Thon had said nothing of this. Did they not know it?

Or had they just decided to keep silent, until the time was right?

He felt in his pocket for the gnomes' farewell gift, pulled out the little Boolong wood box and opened it. "If we send this token, the gnomes will come," he said quietly, as all stared in awe at the golden arrowhead.

"You have powerful friends indeed," breathed Peel.

"Now we have three tribes," said Fardeep, with satisfaction. "What of the others?"

"The Ralads are an ancient race!" Barda exclaimed. "Are they, perhaps — ?"

"Yes," agreed Zeean. "Do you know them?"

"One of them, Manus, helped us to find the ruby at the Lake of Tears," said Barda. "The ruby must have been the Ralad stone!"

Lief searched his jacket again, this time for paper and pencil.

"What of the people of D'Or?" Jasmine asked.

"Their ancestors came to Deltora from across the sea," Doom called over his shoulder. "It was long ago, but after the time of Adin and the seven tribes."

So he is listening after all, thought Lief, scribbling at the list he had begun to make. He pretends to think this is foolishness, but still he cannot move away.

"The Plains people were another tribe," said Zeean. "Their gem was the opal. Then there was the Mere tribe of the upper Broad and beyond — "

"Whose talisman was the lapis lazuli!" Lief broke in, still writing.

Zeean nodded. "The last of the seven, the Jalis, lived in these parts. They were the wildest of all the tribes, and great warriors. Their gem was the diamond."

Lief held up his list.

Tribe	Gem	Where found
1. Del	Topaz (faith)	Forests of Silence
2. Ralad	ruby (happiness)	Lake of tears
3. Plains	Opal (hope)	City of the Rats
4. Mere	lapis lazuli (heavenly stone)	Shifting Sands
5. Dread Gnomes	emerald (honour)	Dread Mountain
6. Tora	amethyst (truth)	Maze of the Beast
7. Jalis	diamond (purity & strength)	Valley of the lost

"All along I have felt that we were being guided on our quest," he said. "Now I am sure of it. We must have met members of all the tribes."

"Except the last. The Jalis," said Jasmine. "We saw no one at all on our way here."

"There was no one to see," said Doom, turning to face them. "When the Shadow Lord came, the Jalis defended their lands ferociously. But even they had no hope against the Grey Guards. They were slaughtered — their children with them. Only a few escaped."

"So you, too, know some history, Doom," said Jasmine pertly.

Doom frowned. "Enough to be sure that if you hope to raise a Jalis army, you will be sadly disappointed."

"We do not want armies," said Zeean. "Armies would be seen and destroyed at once. We need just seven souls — true descendants of the tribes that once allowed their talismans to be joined for the good of all — to put their hands on the Belt, and renew the oath of loyalty to Deltora."

"Yes!" Lief exclaimed, feeling a great surge of hope.

Dain said nothing. But his eyes were shining.

"Torans we have in plenty," Barda said. "Lief and I are of Del. We know Ralads, and Dread Gnomes. But what of the Plains people? The Mere folk? Let alone — "

"I am of the Mere tribe," said Fardeep quietly. He raised his chin as all eyes turned to him. "Rithmere has been my family's home since before the time of Adin."

"What of the Plains people?" asked Peel.

"The people of Noradz must be descended from the Plains tribe," Jasmine murmured. "We have a friend among them — Tira — "

Barda shook his head. "Tira would certainly be killed if she tried to escape Noradz," he said flatly. "Dain? Could your father have been a Plains man?"

"No," Dain said huskily. "Our farm was not far east of here. My father's people were of Del. But . . ." He glanced pleadingly at Doom. Doom sighed, came back to the group and sat down with a weary groan.

"You spoke of fate guiding you," he said to Lief. "I find it hard to believe in such things. But, as it happens, there is a Plains man close by. His family is . . . unusual, but of the Plains nonetheless. I am sure that he would be willing to help. He — and his brother."

Lief's heart sank. "Steven?" he asked faintly.

Doom's face creased into a mocking smile. "And Nevets. For you cannot have one without the other."

"All the better!" exclaimed Fardeep heartily.

Barda, Lief, and Jasmine looked at one another. They were not at all sure of that.

But already Fardeep was speaking again. "Now all that remains is to find a Jalis," he said.

Zeean turned to Doom. "I think that you can help us here, also," she said shrewdly. "I think you were told the Jalis story by one you know. One of the Jalis who escaped. Is that not so?"

Doom's smile broadened. "Indeed it is," he murmured. "And if you want him, you shall have him. He will liven up proceedings, no doubt. Almost as much as Steven will."

"Indeed?" asked Fardeep, beaming.

"Oh, yes. He is a charming fellow," said Doom. "A charming fellow, by the name of Glock."

Barda, Lief, and Jasmine exclaimed in horror.

"We cannot have Glock!" snapped Jasmine.

"Then I fear you cannot have a Jalis," said Doom. "Glock is the only one I have ever seen. The others who escaped are dead, I fear. This is Glock's belief, also."

"Then, whatever this Glock is like, we must ask him to join us," said Zeean quietly. "Where is he now?"

Doom sighed again. "At Withick Mire, a Resistance stronghold near to Del. He was causing trouble where he was. Withick Mire is less — confined."

"So, we have the seven," said Zeean. "Now even you, Doom, must admit that we are being guided."

The lines on Doom's hard face deepened. Then he seemed to come to a decision. "Once you said that when the time was right we would join the fight for Deltora together," he said to Barda. "It seems that time has come. Not, perhaps, in the way I would choose, but —"

"Perhaps we do not even want your help!" snapped Jasmine. "Have you considered that?"

"I cannot say I have," Doom murmured. "I would not think you would be so foolish."

"Indeed we would not," said Barda, frowning at Jasmine, warning her to silence.

Doom's mouth twisted into a wry smile. "Then let us plan," he said. "First, secret messages must be sent to Raladin and Dread Mountain."

"How?" demanded Jasmine.

"You can leave that to me," said Doom. "The Resistance also has useful friends. I suggest the meeting place be Withick Mire."

Lief felt a stirring of unease. Why did Doom want them so close to Del, and their greatest danger?

Because Withick Mire is a Resistance stronghold, the voice of suspicion whispered in his head. *Because there, Doom's word is law.*

Plainly, Barda was also filled with doubt. "Why Withick Mire?" he asked bluntly.

Doom sighed. "It seems that all this will be in vain if we cannot find the heir," he said. "So the closer we are to the possible hiding place, the better. Endon and Sharn were travelling from Del to Tora, but they could not have gone far before they received the Torans' message refusing sanctuary. It was sent at once, I imagine?"

Zeean and Peel nodded, their faces shadowed by this brutal reminder of Tora's broken vow.

But Doom had no time for sparing feelings. "The Kingdom was filled with danger," he went on. "The queen was expecting a child. It is quite likely, then, that the pair sought refuge nearby — somewhere between Del and the Valley of the Lost."

A shiver ran up Lief's spine. Their quest had

taken them in a great circle, bringing them back to the area where the heir was most likely to be. Somewhere to the west of Del. A quiet place, where Endon and Sharn could bring up their child unnoticed.

Something twitched at the corner of his mind. A memory of something he had heard, not very long ago. He could not quite catch hold of it . . .

"But surely it is better to remain here," Fardeep was arguing. "If Lief, Barda, and Jasmine move from hiding, they will draw the Shadow Lord's attention."

"We can travel hidden in Steven's caravan," said Jasmine, who was plainly burning for action. "Besides, despite Doom's doubts, we are certain the Shadow Lord's search is being concentrated in the west."

"Perhaps we can make doubly sure." Doom swung around to Peel. "You are about Barda's height and coloring. And among your people there must be two who resemble these young ones," he said, pointing at Lief and Jasmine.

Peel nodded silently, his eyebrows raised.

"We need decoys," Doom explained. "To show themselves near the River Tor. A girl, a boy, and a man, a blackbird flying with them. Steven can provide clothes that will — "

"No! It is too dangerous!" exclaimed Jasmine.

"Are you the only ones who must face danger?" Peel asked gently. "The plan is clever. And it is fitting that Torans should carry it out. If we must live in exile, we can at least try to repair the great wrong that caused it."

"One day you will be able to go back to Tora," Lief cried, his heart torn. "The heir's forgiveness will surely undo the curse."

Zeean raised her head. "Perhaps," she said gravely. "But first the heir must be found. And we will do our part." She looked carefully at Lief and Jasmine. "Your friend Steven will not have a cloak like that," she said to Lief. "The cloth is very rare. Worthy of the looms of Tora. How did you come by it?"

"My mother made it for me." Lief touched the rough fabric of his cloak.

Zeean's eyebrows rose in surprise, and Lief felt a flicker of pleasure mixed with pain. Pride at his mother's skill. Fear for her.

✳

The rest of the day passed in a blur. When Lief thought of it afterwards, he remembered only pictures:

Dain hurrying away to fetch Steven. Fardeep packing food. The eager faces of Kris and Lauran, the young Torans chosen as the decoys. Lauran having her silky hair curled and tangled so that it looked like Jasmine's. Kris's long black hair being cut to match Lief's own. The golden arrowhead on the palm of his own hand. Blackbirds waiting silently in the trees.

Then Steven's cart trundling through the valley. Steven nodding, studying the message Barda had written. Steven sitting alone by Fardeep's beehives, murmuring, drawing in the dust. The bees swarming up through the mist that shrouded the treetops, and speeding towards Broad River . . .

Evening. Three people moving into the clearing. A big, roughly bearded man, a boy wearing a long cloak, and a wild-looking girl, a blackbird on her arm. Like looking in a mirror. Doom nodding with satisfaction. Zeean, very proud and upright, her eyes dark with fear. Peel, Kris, and Lauran embracing their families before slipping away to begin their perilous journey . . .

Night. Air thick and hard to breathe. The slow slipping into sleep, and dreams. Dreams of desperate searching. Of legs that could not run. Of tied hands and blinded eyes. Of veiled faces and smiling masks that slipped aside to reveal writhing horrors. And, brooding over all, a crawling mass of scarlet and grey, the darkness at its center pulsing with malice.

Calling him.

5 - Messages

The caravan jolted on the rough road. Inside, it was dim and stuffy. Hour after hour Lief, Barda, and Jasmine sat, listening to the sounds of jingling reins, creaking wheels, and two voices singing.

Do I spy an Ol-io,
Ol-io, Ol-io?
Hello, wobbly Ol-io!
You don't bother me!

It had been decided that it would attract too much attention if the whole party travelled together. Dain, Doom, Fardeep, and Zeean were moving overland.

"Steven and Nevets are more than capable of defending you, if need be," Doom had said.

Lief was sure this was true. Still, his skin crept as he thought of the strange brothers singing together on the driver's seat at the front of the caravan.

Barda, like the trained soldier he was, had taken the chance to sleep. Propped against a pile of rugs, he dozed as comfortably as if he were in a soft bed. But Jasmine was wide awake. Kree hunched beside her, his feathers ruffled indignantly. Filli slept inside her jacket. She frowned as the singing voices were raised once more.

"It is all very well to be jolly," she muttered. "But must they sing such nonsense?"

Lief sighed agreement. Despite himself, he found he was following the foolish words.

Time to stop and take the air,
Ol-io, Ol-io.
Trees ahead, the sky is clear,
No more Ol-io!

Lief sat bolt upright, his eyes widening. He had suddenly realized that the song was far from nonsense. All along, Steven had been sending them messages!

"Soon we will be able to get out and stretch our legs," he told Jasmine gleefully. "There are trees ahead, and no sign of Ols or Ak-Baba."

Jasmine stared at him, her frown deepening. Plainly, she thought he was losing his wits.

✳

Far away, a round old woman, her face as red and crinkled as a wizened apple, bent over clear water. Around her head swarmed a black cloud of bees.

The woman was listening. Large silver fish hung in the water below her. Bubbles streamed from their mouths, making strange patterns on the surface.

At last, the woman straightened and turned, settling her many shawls around her shoulders. The bees swirled before her. The patterns they made in the air mimicked the trails of bubbles that marked the water.

"So," she said to them. "You have learned your lesson well. Passed on from your sister bees in the south, to the fish, to you. Go, then!"

And the bees were off, a humming black arrow, carrying the message on.

✳

Jinks emerged from the Resistance stronghold of the west and shivered in the cold wind. The sky was clear except for a flock of blackbirds, dark specks against the blue. Jinks shaded his eyes and peered at them.

Birds? Or Ols? Ols did not usually fly so high. But, on the other hand, the flock was heading for Dread Mountain. And what real bird would go there?

Suddenly Jinks saw a tiny flash in the center of the flock — as if the sun had struck something made of bright metal. But what would an Ol — or a bird, for that matter — be doing carrying such a thing?

My eyes are deceiving me. I must be tired, Jinks thought. Yawning, he returned to the cavern.

✳

Tom the shopkeeper was serving ale to Grey Guards in the little tavern he kept beside his shop.

"There are many of you about at present," he said lightly. "Some of your fellows were here only yesterday."

One of the Guards grunted, reaching for a brimming mug. "They are ordered to the west," he said. "And many others, too. We are to stay in the northeast, worse luck. We will miss the real fighting."

"Fighting?" Tom's lean face creased into a broad smile as he passed the other mugs around.

"You talk too much, Teep 4," grunted a second guard.

Tom raised his eyebrows. "Old Tom is no threat!" he exclaimed. "What is he but a poor shopkeeper?"

"A poor innkeeper, too!" snarled Teep 4. "This ale tastes like muddlet droppings."

Amid loud guffaws, the shop bell sounded. Tom excused himself and went through a door, closing it behind him. Waiting in the shop were a man and a woman, well muffled against the cold.

"Greetings! How can I serve you?" Tom asked.

Without a word, the woman made a mark on the dust of the counter.

Tom casually swept the mark away as he pulled a package from under the counter. "This is your order, I believe," he said. He gave the package to the woman, then glanced quickly at the tavern door.

"I have news," he murmured. The customers bent towards him, and he began speaking rapidly.

❋

High on Dread Mountain, Gla-Thon saw a flock of blackbirds approaching and fitted an arrow to her bow.

The gnomes still placed filled glass bottles at the base of the mountain for the Grey Guards to take to the Shadowlands. The fact that the liquid in the bottles was now water and Boolong sap instead of deadly poison was something the Guards would discover only when they tried to use the blisters made from it.

Perhaps, at last, that time had come. Perhaps the blackbirds were the first sign that the Shadow Lord had discovered the Dread Gnomes' treachery.

If so, we are ready, thought Gla-Thon grimly. She heard rustling behind her and spun around. But it was only Prin, the youngest of the Kin.

"Birds!" Prin gasped. "Blackbirds — "

"I have seen them," grunted Gla-Thon.

The flock was wheeling close, now. Gla-Thon's arrow strained against her bowstring. Then one of the birds separated from the rest and plunged towards her. In its beak was something that flashed golden in the sun.

And even before the bird had landed, Gla-Thon was shouting. Shouting that the sign had come.

✳

Manus lifted his head from his work in the vegetable beds of Raladin to swat the flies that were swarming around him. Then he stared.

The flies were not flies at all, but bees. The air seemed full of them. As Manus watched, easing his aching back, he frowned.

The bees were acting strangely. They were not hovering around the flowers, but buzzing in the sky. They were clustering together, making patterns. And the patterns . . .

Manus's jaw dropped. The spade fell from his hand. With his long, blue-grey finger he began tracing in the soil the patterns the bees were making, black against the blue.

Manus sat back on his heels and read what he had written. The message was clear. "One person — travel to — friends — quickly. For freedom!"

✳

Many days passed. Slow days for Lief, Barda, and Jasmine, cooped up in the caravan. They knew from Steven's songs that Ak-Baba had flown overhead and Ols in all shapes had stared as the caravan passed by. But the caravan was a familiar sight to the Ak-Baba, and the Ols were not interested in it. They had been ordered to keep watch — but not for that.

> *Road forks just ahead I see,*
> *Ol-io, Ol-io!*
> *Night is falling, we seem free*
> *Of Ol-i, Ol-ios!*

Steven was singing again, giving the news.

A few minutes later, the caravan stopped, the back doors were thrown open, and the companions scrambled out. It was just past sunset. A rocky hill rose in front of them. The main road curved around the hill to the right. Another track wound off to the left. A signpost stood at the fork. Lief's throat tightened as he read it.

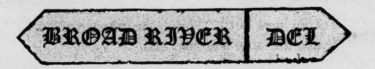

BROAD RIVER | DEL

"We must take the Del road, but it will be a journey into the unknown," said Steven. "I know nothing of it, and neither does Doom. He always travels overland in these parts. The hills that hide the coast are treacherous, he says. But he prefers them."

"I would prefer them, also," muttered Jasmine.

"And I," growled Barda. "But we must stay hidden. If we are sighted here, the decoys in the west will have risked their lives to no purpose."

Lief was looking at the Del road. Endon and Sharn had no doubt followed it from the city, the night they escaped. They would not have tried to go overland, with Sharn so close to giving birth to her child.

He tried to imagine how it would have been. The road would have been crowded. Many fled from Del that night. He remembered his father's sad voice, telling him about it. "Your mother and I stayed shut up in the forge all through the uproar. When at last we opened our gates, we found ourselves alone. Friends, neighbors, old customers — all were gone. Killed, captured, or fled."

"We had been expecting something of the sort," Lief's mother had added. "But the confusion was worse than even we had imagined. It took a long time for life in Del to begin again. When it did, we were ready. And so grateful — because we were safe, and so were you, my son, for by that time you had been born, and were the light of our lives. But . . ." Her strong voice trembled. "But we feared for those who had fled."

Those who had fled.

Unrecognized in their humble working clothes, Endon and Sharn would have lost themselves in the panicking crowd. They would have hurried along with others moving west, suffering who knew what terrors. Then, when the blackbird carrying Tora's message reached them, they would have realized that there was no point in continuing.

What would they have done then? Moved off the road. Found a place to hide. Endon knew the Belt would never again shine for him. Deltora's only hope lay with his child. He and Sharn had to find a place where the baby could be born in safety. Where?

Lief was roused by Jasmine's sharp voice. "Lief! We must go, so we can find a place to stop for the night."

Lief turned to the caravan. But his thoughts still dwelled on a time before he was born, and on two desperate people he had never known, searching for refuge.

6 ~ Dangerous Road

Rain threatened as they set off the next day. The companions cared nothing for that, cheered by Steven's assurance that they would reach Withick Mire before sunset. But they had not gone far before his voice reached them with bad news.

> *Be prepared for flight or fight.*
> *Ol-io, Ol-io!*
> *Gripper field lies to the right,*
> *Ahead are Guard-ios.*

"What is a gripper field?" whispered Jasmine, as the caravan jerked to a stop.

"It cannot be worse than Grey Guards, in any case," growled Barda. "And Guards, it seems, are ahead."

The caravan doors were thrown open, and Steven looked in.

"The road is blocked," he hissed. "The Guards must be searching all carts that pass." He heaved a barrel from a corner as Lief, Barda, and Jasmine scrambled out onto the road. They were hidden from the Guards because the caravan had stopped in the middle of a bend. But once it moved on . . .

Lief looked quickly for a way of escape. On one side was sheer, high rock. On the other was a field, bordered by thickly wooded hills.

"Make for the hills," muttered Steven. "With luck, the Guards will not notice you. We will meet further on. Take care. The stones are hard to — "

He broke off as a hoarse shout came from the road ahead. He slammed the doors and moved to the front of the caravan, carrying the barrel. "I am coming, sirs," he called. "With ale, for your pleasure."

The companions heard him climb onto the driver's seat. Then the caravan began to move.

Kree soared towards the hills. Lief, Barda, and Jasmine rolled into the ditch that edged the road.

"I see no sign of grippers, whatever they may be," Barda whispered, scanning the field.

Indeed, the field appeared quite empty. The only unusual thing about it was its bright green color, caused by a multitude of large, flat weeds. Like round mats made up of circles of broad leaves, the weeds pressed closely together, almost choking out the grass.

Lief glanced along the road. The caravan had almost reached the Guards. There were ten — a whole pod. The road was blocked by fallen trees. Heaps of rubbish, empty barrels, and boxes lay everywhere. Plainly, the Guards had been on duty here for months.

They will be bored, eager for entertainment, Lief thought, his heart sinking.

"And what do we have here?" one of the Guards shouted. "A big, ugly tick with a horse to match!" There was a gale of laughter as his brothers gathered around the caravan, their eyes fixed on Steven.

"Now!" hissed Barda.

Keeping together under the shelter of Lief's cloak, the companions began scrambling forward. But almost at once Barda staggered, with a muffled cry of pain. At the same moment, Jasmine gasped and fell to her knees.

Lief whirled around, crouching to help them. But when he put down his left hand to brace himself, the ground gave way beneath it, and his hand was dragged down by something that bit and burned.

His hand had sunk into the center of one of the flat weeds. The center was widening, sucking at his arm, drawing it down . . .

Wildly, Lief tore himself free. His hand was covered in blood. The center of the plant gaped like a huge, flabby-lipped mouth, flecked with red. With horror, Lief looked down at the rows of vicious teeth lining the green throat that plunged deep into the earth.

The plants! Grippers! Steven thought we knew . . .

Beside him, Jasmine struggled to free her trapped leg as Filli squealed in terror, trying vainly to help her, and Kree flew back to her side. Barda floundered in agony behind them, both legs caught and sinking.

Lief seized Jasmine's arms and heaved. Her leg came free dripping blood, and all around her grippers opened their hideous mouths wide. Cheers rang out from the road, and for a moment Lief thought they had been seen. But when he looked, he saw that the Guards had their backs to the field. They were gathered around the barrel, filling their mugs.

"Barda!" choked Jasmine. Barda was pinned to the ground. All four of his limbs were trapped, now. His neck strained as he fought to hold his face away from a pulsing, greedy green mouth gaping just below it. Every moment he sank deeper, deeper . . .

Why am I not sinking? thought Lief. He looked down. He was standing on a patch of pale grass. Then he realized that the grass was covering a flat stone. Steven had begun to say something about stones . . .

The stones are hard to — to see!

With a moan of frustration Lief saw pale patches making a line through the field. Stepping stones! A path that would always be safe because, though grass could overgrow a stone, grippers could only grow in deep earth.

He and Jasmine were standing on stones right

now. Barda lay in a seething mass of bright green. But the line of stones snaked beside him.

"Jasmine! The pale patches are safe!" Lief hissed. "Move back along them!" As she sprang to obey, he snatched his rope from his belt and followed.

When he reached her, Jasmine was stabbing viciously at the grippers holding Barda. The plants were quivering and recoiling a little. Lief pushed the end of the rope under Barda's chest. Then, leaning over perilously, he pulled it through on the other side and knotted it, pulling it tight under the big man's arms.

"Help me, Barda!" he gasped, pulling with all his might. And Barda, making a final, anguished effort, groaned and arched his body.

His arms came free. The sleeves of his jacket were torn to ribbons, soaked with blood. The greedy mouths beneath him yawned wide.

Her teeth bared in disgust, Jasmine began attacking the leaves around Barda's trapped legs. Again Lief heaved on the rope. This time Barda could help little. Blood flowed freely from his torn flesh, and he had almost lost consciousness. But at last, with agonizing slowness, his legs began to ease out of the ground, till he was free.

Jasmine and Lief rolled him onto the stepping stones and began half carrying, half dragging him towards the hills.

The noise from the road rose to a gleeful roar. The Guards had thought of a new entertainment. Five of them were holding Steven at dagger's point. The other five were pulling the horse towards the gripper field. The creature, sensing its danger, was rearing and plunging, screaming in terror.

The Guards were cheering. Steven was shouting at them to stop, to stop! His huge brown figure with its crown of golden hair was almost hidden in a jostling crowd of grey uniforms.

Lief's blood ran cold. "Jasmine, faster!" he cried. The trees were not far away now. A few more steps . . .

There was a spine-chilling bellow. Lief looked up. The Guards were falling to the ground, their hands pressed to their eyes. Steven was staggering back, blinding yellow light pouring from his body like smoke. Then another figure was rising in front of him, taking shape in the glare. A golden giant, with a wild mane of dark brown hair.

"Nevets," Lief whispered.

The giant's body was covered in golden fur. His yellow eyes glittered with cruel fury. His massive fingers were tipped with viciously curved brown claws. He lunged for the terrified horse and swung it to safety. Then, growling like a beast, he began snatching up the screaming, writhing Guards, shaking them like dolls, and tearing them apart.

Lief and Jasmine stood frozen in horror. Steven crawled to his feet, and saw them. "Go!" he roared. "Once he has begun, I cannot stop him! Get out of his sight!"

✳

Safe under the trees, Lief and Jasmine bandaged Barda's terrible wounds, wrapped him in blankets, and gave him Queen Bee honey. But the bleeding would not stop, and Barda did not stir. Rain began, soaking, icy.

Desperately, Lief looked for shelter. Then he gave a cry of amazement. Not far away, like the answer to a prayer, was an old stone hut, almost hidden by bushes. Of course! The stepping stones had once led to someone's home.

With Kree fluttering anxiously above them, Lief and Jasmine hauled Barda to the hut. Inside, it was dark, for the small windows were filmed with dirt. There was a musty, unpleasant smell. But it was dry, and its fireplace was piled with sticks and dead grass.

They dragged Barda inside and Jasmine ran to the fireplace. In moments she had started a fire. The tinder-dry wood crackled as flames leaped up. Light began to flicker around the tiny room.

And it was then that Lief saw what lay in a corner.

Two skeletons were propped against the wall. Scraps of clothing still clung to the bones, and hair to the skulls, so Lief could see that it had been a man and a woman who had crept in here to die. Then he saw that the woman cradled in her arms, in the tatters of a shawl, another small heap of bones — the bones of a tiny baby.

Sweat broke out on his forehead. He forced himself to take a step forward, then another. There was something lying at the man's feet. A flat tin box.

"No!" Jasmine's hushed voice was filled with fear, but Lief did not stop. He picked up the box and opened it. Inside was a scrap of parchment covered in black writing. He squinted at it, the terrible words dancing before his eyes. He took a deep, shuddering breath.

"What is it?" whispered Jasmine.

Lief read the note aloud. His voice sounded thin, like the voice of someone he did not know.

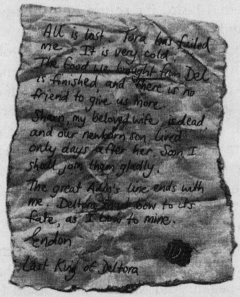

All is lost. Tora has failed me. It is very cold. The food we brought from Del is finished, and there is no friend to give us more. Sharn, my beloved wife, is dead, and our newborn son lived only days after her. Soon I shall join them gladly.

The great Adin's line ends with me. Deltora shall bow to its fate, as I bow to mine.

Endon
Last King of Deltora

The note crushed in his hand, Lief stared at the bones. He could not take in what he was seeing.

The heir to Deltora was not safe in hiding, waiting for them. The heir had been dead all along.

"This Endon was a man who did not deserve to be king," Jasmine said harshly. "Weak and peevish, filled with pity for himself. It is what I always feared."

Lief forced himself to speak. "You are cruel, Jasmine!" he whispered. "He had lost all he loved when he wrote this note. He was in despair."

"He caused his loss himself!" Jasmine spat. "If he had been brave enough to depend on himself for once, they would have survived, as my parents did. There is wood here. I heard the sound of a stream. There are berries and other wild foods."

She shook her head angrily. "But oh, no! Still looking for others to hold his hand and make his life easy, he could not even try to help himself or his family. And so they ended in this barren place, starving and cold, and his wife and her little one died." Her eyes were brimming with tears as she stared at the tiny, ragged bundle resting on the woman's breast.

"We will never know the truth of it," Lief said heavily. "But one thing we do know. Without the heir to wear it, the Belt cannot save Deltora."

His chest was tight, his stomach churning. Barda is dying, he thought. Dying for a cause that was lost before it began. And Mother and Father! How much have they suffered? All for nothing. Nothing! Father's plan to help his friend and hide the heir led only to death and misery. Who told him the lie that the Belt would remain whole only while the heir lived?

Was it stated in *The Belt of Deltora*? Lief searched his memory. No! He was sure — positive — that the little book had never mentioned any such thing. Why had he not thought of that before?

Because I simply believed what Father told me, he thought dismally. As no doubt Father believed someone else. Prandine, perhaps. Or even Endon himself. He bowed his head, in an agony of despair.

7 – Withick Mire

The caravan swayed. The bells on the reins jingled. But Steven was not singing. Inside, in the dimness, Lief and Jasmine sat with Barda lying between them, trying to protect their injured friend from the worst of the jolts.

They had spent a miserable hour by the hut fire before Steven came looking for them. Lief shivered, remembering what had happened when Steven saw the skeletons and read the note.

Steven's face had darkened. His face had begun to heave. Suddenly he had screwed his eyes shut and pressed his lips together. "No! No!" Lief heard him mutter as he turned away, beating the stone wall with his fists. And Lief knew he was struggling with Nevets, trying to keep his savage brother in check.

After a few moments, the battle was won. Steven turned back to them, his face weary, but calm. "What cannot be changed, must be endured," he said grimly. "Our duty now is to the living."

He bent over Barda. "Ah — this is my fault," he murmured. "I thought you knew of gripper fields."

"Will Barda live?" Lief's throat was tight as he asked the question.

Steven gnawed at his lip, hesitating. "At Withick Mire he will be warm and comfortable," he said finally.

He bent and lifted Barda as easily as if the big man were a child. Then he strode from the hut without a backward glance. Lief and Jasmine trailed after him, both very aware that he had not answered the question.

They walked in silence through the trees to where the stepping stones began, then picked their way back across the gripper field. Ahead, the caravan stood alone, the horse waiting beside it. The trees that had blocked the road had been cast aside. The cooking fires, the stores, and the rubbish had been swept away as though blown by a great wind.

Of the Guards there was no sign except for a few scraps of bloodstained grey fabric scattered here and there. With a chill Lief realized that Nevets had chosen the easiest way to dispose of the remains of his victims. The grippers closest to the road had been well fed.

✳

Hours later, they began to notice a vile smell. The stench of rot and decay seeped into the caravan till the still, dusty air was thick with it. Jasmine wrinkled her nose in disgust. "What is it?" she whispered.

Lief shrugged, then steadied himself as the caravan rocked violently as though it was travelling over rough ground.

He looked down at Barda. The rough bandages that bound Barda's legs and arms were soaked with blood. He had taken a little water, and when they smeared Queen Bee honey on his mouth, he licked it from his lips. But he had not opened his eyes or spoken.

The honey is all that is keeping him alive, Lief thought. But for how long? How long? Oh, let us reach Withick Mire soon!

So that Barda could be cared for properly. So that his wounds could be washed and freshly bandaged. So that — Lief forced himself to think of it — so that if Barda had to die, he could die peacefully, comfortably, on a warm couch, instead of in this cold, shaking, stinking caravan.

At that very moment, to his surprise, the caravan came to a stop. The back doors were flung open, and Lief and Jasmine scrambled out.

The rain had stopped. The sun was setting, flooding the sky with dull orange light that lit a strange and horrible scene. The caravan was in the middle of a giant garbage dump. Giant, stinking mounds of rags, bones, broken furniture, and household goods, twisted metal and rotting food scraps rose on all sides. Among the mounds, ragged, miserable people bent and shuffled, searching the refuse.

Lief spun around angrily to Steven. "Why have you brought us here?" he demanded. "We must get Barda to Withick Mire!"

Without a word Steven pointed at a sign that stood just beside where the caravan had stopped.

Before Lief could say anything, one of the ragged scavengers came shambling towards them, leaning heavily on a stick. A black patch covered one of his eyes and he had tied a scarf around his mouth and nose, no doubt to protect him from the stench of the mounds. He bent forward, leering at the newcomers with his one good eye.

"What do you seek here, may I ask?" he rasped, his voice just a croak. "Here, amid the leavings of Del?"

Lief and Jasmine hesitated, not knowing what to say.

The scavenger cackled. "Perhaps you seek shelter?" he asked. "Then come with me. All are welcome in Withick Mire."

He hobbled off, threading his way through the mounds with the ease of long practice. Not knowing what else to do, the companions followed, Lief and Jasmine on foot, Steven leading the horse carefully through the maze.

As they walked, they passed many pathetic hovels made of pieces of wood, tin, and cloth. People crouched outside these hovels, sorting through the pickings of the day, or starting cooking fires. Some grinned up at the strangers. Others did not bother to raise their heads.

At the back of one of the larger mounds, a more substantial shelter had been built. The scavenger beckoned, and Lief and Jasmine, with a backward glance at Steven, followed him inside.

And there a surprise awaited them. Beneath the thin layer of tin and board was a sturdy building. It was far larger than it had appeared from the outside, because all but its entry was buried deep under the mound. It was not only large, but clean and well organized, with many stretchers arranged neatly around the walls, each topped with folded blankets, and with possessions stacked below.

The scavenger turned to them, straightened, and threw off both the eye patch and the scarf.

"Doom!" Jasmine exclaimed in amazement.

"Did you not know me?" asked Doom, his lips

tweaking into a smile. "That is excellent! You did not expect the Resistance stronghold to be in a garbage dump, no doubt. But what better place to hide? No one comes here willingly — not even Grey Guards. And who cares for or about poor scavengers? Some of the people you saw on your way here are true scavengers — sad souls from Del whose livelihoods have been taken from them. Others — many others — are our people. Glock, Fardeep, and even Zeean are out there somewhere, with all the rest. Dain is away fetching water."

Leif nodded slowly, taking it in. So nothing is as it seems, even here, he thought.

"Doom," Jasmine said urgently. "Barda is injured. He needs care. And . . ." She glanced at Lief. "There is other news. Very bad."

Lief fumbled in his pocket and drew out Endon's crumpled note.

Doom's dark eyes grew even darker as though, somehow, he knew what was coming. But he did not take the note. Instead, he turned swiftly to face the door once more.

"Time enough for that when Barda has been seen to," he said roughly. "Bring him in. We will do what we can for him."

✳

Later, Lief and Jasmine sat by Barda's bed. Their own wounds had been washed and bandaged, and the big man lay peacefully at last. The bleeding had stopped, and for this they had to thank a strange ally — Glock.

"You won't heal this with bandages," Glock had mumbled, grabbing Lief's wrist and inspecting it. "Grippers inject something that keeps the blood flowing."

He went over to his own stretcher, rummaged beneath it, then came back holding a grubby jar filled with grey paste. "Smear this on the bites," he ordered.

"What is it?" asked Jasmine, smelling the paste suspiciously.

"How would I know?" snarled Glock. "Those who made it are long dead. But my tribe always used it in the old days — for half-wits and infants who blundered into gripper fields."

Jasmine bit back her angry response and turned to Barda.

"Do not waste it on him," Glock growled. "He is finished."

Jasmine did not bother to reply. Already she was smearing the paste on Barda's cleaned wounds. Glock spat in disgust, and lumbered away. Now he was nowhere to be seen.

Lief looked up wearily. Zeean, Fardeep, and Doom were standing together not far away, with Steven beside them. Their heads were bent. Their faces were grave. They were reading Endon's note.

"So," Lief heard Doom say heavily. "That is the end of that."

They looked up, saw Lief and Jasmine watching, and moved to join them. Doom handed the note back to Lief.

"The Dread Gnome and the Ralad will arrive to find they have made their journey for nothing," he said.

Lief nodded. "All our journeys have been for nothing," he replied through stiff lips.

Zeean's face was shadowed with grief. "It is very hard," she murmured. "I had — such hopes."

"It is well for our hopes to be dashed, if they were false." The old bitterness had returned to Doom's voice. "Soon we will all return to our places. And every step we go, we will tell what we know, so no other fools will be tempted to risk their lives in a useless cause."

There was a sound beside Lief. He looked down, and his heart thudded. Barda had stirred. His eyes were open.

"What is — the matter?" Barda asked weakly.

Jasmine stroked his forehead. "Nothing is the matter," she said soothingly. "Rest, now."

But Barda moved his head impatiently and his eyes fastened on the note in Lief's hand. "What is that? Show it to me!" he demanded.

Lief knew Barda too well to think he could refuse. Reluctantly, he held out the note so that Barda could see it, explaining how it had been found.

Barda blinked at the terrible words. Then, to

Lief's amazement, he smiled. "And — is this what is troubling you?" he asked.

Lief and Jasmine exchanged alarmed glances. Barda's mind was wandering. Jasmine bent over the bed once more. "Sleep," she whispered. "You need rest, Barda. You are very weak."

"Weak I may be," Barda said softly. "But not so weak that I do not know a falsehood when I see it."

8 - Arrivals

Barda gazed wearily up at the ring of astounded faces, and again he smiled. "The note is a good forgery, oh, yes," he murmured. "The writing is very like that on the note we saw in Tora. But the mind that framed these words was not Endon's mind. I — "

His voice faltered as he was distracted by a noise. Lief quickly turned to see Dain hurrying towards them from the door, his eyes wide with questions. But before the boy could speak, Doom frowned and raised his finger to his lips. Lief turned back to the bed.

"How can you tell the note was not written by King Endon, Barda?" Jasmine asked gently. "You did not know him."

"Perhaps not," muttered Barda. "But Jarred did. Time and again Jarred has told me of Endon's terrible feelings of guilt. It brought tears into his own eyes to tell of Endon's agony when he realized how he had failed Deltora. Yet this, which is supposed to be Endon's last message, written not long after the escape from Del, says not one word of that."

"You are right." Lief felt that he was slowly waking from a nightmare. "Not one word of apology or grief for anyone other than for himself and his family. And this cannot be. The note — the skeletons — were planted to deceive us! That is why the Guards were placed where they were. To force travellers off the road, up to the hut. It was all a Shadow Lord plan."

I have many plans . . .

"But . . ." Like Jasmine, Doom was plainly not convinced.

Barda tossed his head restlessly. "Look at the seal at the bottom of the message. It should not be there. The note in Tora did not bear the royal seal. And why? Because Endon did not have the seal ring in his possession when he escaped. He could not have done so. The seal was always kept by Prandine, and brought out only when messages had to be signed."

"How do you know this?" asked Zeean curiously.

Barda sighed. "My mother, rest her soul, was nursemaid to both Jarred and Endon. She was a great chatterer, and told me many things about palace doings. Often I only half listened, I admit. But it seems that I learned more than the Shadow Lord suspects."

"And what a blessing you did," breathed Far-deep, his eyes goggling. "If it had not been for you, we would have abandoned all our hopes."

"I have stayed alive to some purpose, then," said Barda, with the faintest of smiles. "But now I am very weary." His eyes closed.

Jasmine drew a sharp breath and pressed her ear to his chest. When she straightened, her face was very pale. "He is only asleep," she whispered. "But his heart beats very faintly. I fear he is slipping away from us."

Blindly she put out her hand to Lief, and he clasped it, his eyes filling with tears. How much our journey has changed us, he thought, dazed with grief. Jasmine shows feeling, and reaches out for comfort! I am not ashamed to weep! How Barda would smile at that.

Steven touched his arm. "Do not grieve before you must, my friend," he said gently. "Barda is strong, and a fighter. He will not give up easily. And Queen Bee honey has performed miracles before."

Lief felt Jasmine's hand tighten on his own. Then there was a sudden movement beside him. He looked around and saw that Dain had pushed his way to the bed, and was kneeling at his side. The boy's eyes were wet, but his face was determined. "Barda must not die," he said. "If we tend him carefully, surely he will recover."

Jasmine's face was glowing with gratitude as she

looked at Dain. But this time Lief felt no jealous pang. If Barda was to be saved, he needed all the hope and help he could get.

✳

That night, and another day, passed in a dream. Lief, Jasmine, and Dain watched over Barda in turns, coaxing him to take honey, water, and spoonfuls of broth. At times Barda seemed to strengthen a little, rousing himself and even speaking. But soon the weakness would take hold again, and before long he would be worse than ever.

It was as if he was on a gradual downward slide that could not be halted. The stirrings were coming less often now.

Barda is dying, Lief told himself. I must face it. But still he could not make himself give up hope. Jasmine certainly had not. And Dain was a tower of strength, taking longer and longer turns at the bedside, sparing them as much as he could.

At sunset, Lief had just stood up from the bedside, giving up his place to Dain, when a shrill cry was heard outside.

"Ak-Baba! Beware!"

Suddenly all was confusion as people began streaming through the door into the shelter. Lief looked around frantically. Where was Jasmine?

Then he remembered. Jasmine had gone with Zeean and Fardeep to collect water. He pushed his way through the throng in the doorway and ran out-

68

side. Almost at once he saw the three he was seeking. They were standing with brimming pails, looking upward at the dark shadow approaching through the orange glare of the sky.

"Jasmine!" Lief shouted. "Run!"

But to his surprise Jasmine simply turned and smiled wearily at him. He looked up once more, then realized what the shadow was.

It was no Ak-Baba. It was a Kin! Ailsa, if he was not mistaken. She was surrounded by a wavering cloud of blackbirds. As they came over the Mire, the birds swooped away and Ailsa began dropping to earth. A small figure in her pouch was waving vigorously.

Gla-Thon, Lief guessed, squinting up at the sky and waving back. Quick-thinking, sharp-tongued Gla-Thon. He recognized her sturdy body, her frizz of brown hair. And who but Gla-Thon would have thought of asking a Kin to fly her speedily to the meeting? Old Fa-Glin may have agreed to make peace with the gnomes' Kin neighbors. But Lief thought it unlikely that he would have consented to ride with one.

Now six of the seven tribes are represented here, Lief thought, as he ran with Jasmine to welcome the newcomers. I should be excited. I should be filled with hope.

And in a way he was. Celebration, and much talk, would follow this arrival, he knew. He looked forward to explaining everything to Gla-Thon. He was overjoyed to see Ailsa again. But the fear of losing Barda hung over him like a cloud, blurring every thought, every feeling.

✳

A few days later, Lief was sitting beside Barda's bed, half drowsing, when there was a light touch on his shoulder. Startled, he spun around and met two solemn black button eyes set in a wrinkled blue-grey face.

"Manus!" he exclaimed, leaping up and bending to fling his arms around the Ralad man. "Oh, Manus! You came!"

"Of course," said Manus. He turned to the golden-maned man standing behind him, with Jasmine. "Our friend Nanion, chief of D'Or, was the means of my arriving so quickly. Nanion has a way with horses which I do not. His feet reach the stirrups, for one thing! But I must say it was an uncomfortable journey. I was terrified half out of my life, and bruised from head to toe!"

Nanion laughed. "To follow a swarm of bees over rough country is no easy task," he said. "And this Ralad complained from the beginning of the journey to the end. I am relieved to have arrived at last, and to be free of his nagging." But his eyes were warm as he spoke. Plainly, he and Manus had become good friends.

"How did you come to have a horse?" Jasmine asked. "And such a fine one!"

Nanion shrugged. "A certain shopkeeper made it available to me," he said. "I only hope he has a good explanation ready for its owners when they come seeking it."

"I daresay he has," said Doom dryly, strolling up behind them. "Good explanations are Tom's specialty. So — he finally decided to take sides, did he?"

Manus smiled. "Not quite that, I think," he said. "He warned Nanion that lightning does not strike twice in the same place. Meaning, I suppose, that we should expect no more favors from him."

"But I think he had forgotten that he had already done us one good turn," Nanion put in. "Shortly before I saw him, he had given two of my people some news. Grey Guards are being ordered to the west. Fighting is expected."

Doom's eyebrows shot up. "Indeed?" he muttered. He drew Nanion aside, leaving Manus alone with Barda, Lief, and Jasmine.

"This is a sorrowful thing," Manus murmured, looking down at the big man lying so still on the bed. "Can nothing be done?"

Lief shook his head. "He has not stirred since sunrise," he said, all his grief flooding back. "I think — it cannot be long."

Manus bowed his head. "Then I am glad I arrived when I did," he said softly. "For it means much to me to see him again. He has a great heart."

He looked up, meeting Lief's eyes squarely. "He

has not given his life in vain," he said. "Jasmine has told me why I was summoned, though I think I had already guessed. You three have worked a miracle."

"Part of a miracle," Lief answered. "The heir is still to be found."

"And is that not why we are all here?" Manus asked quietly. He stood up. "The moon is rising. It is time for the seven tribes to join once more. It is time for the heir to be summoned."

9 – The Heir

Candles flickered around the walls. Faces — grave, excited, afraid — formed a half circle around the seven. All eyes were on the Belt, lying in shadow, on the table where Lief had set it.

They were standing by Barda's bed. Jasmine had insisted on that. "In whatever twilight world he is wandering, he may hear us," she said. "And even if he cannot, it is his right to be present."

No one argued with her. But it was clear to all that Barda's long struggle for life was almost done.

Zeean stepped forward. "I, Zeean of Tora, am here," she said gravely, laying her hand upon the amethyst.

Gla-Thon was next. "And I, Gla-Thon of the Dread Gnomes," she said, her head held high as she caressed the emerald.

Lief watched, holding himself rigidly, as one by one the others moved forward.

"Fardeep, of the Mere." Fardeep's usually hearty voice was shaking. Humbly, he touched the lapis lazuli.

"Steven, of the Plains." Steven towered over all the rest, his golden hair gleaming as he bent to the opal.

"Manus, for the Ralad people." Manus brushed the ruby with gentle fingers.

Glock lumbered forward. His face was fierce and proud as he stretched out his huge paw to the diamond. "I am Glock, last of the Jalis," he growled. And Lief caught his breath as he saw tears spring into the savage eyes.

Then it was his turn. He squeezed Barda's hand and moved to the Belt. The faces of the watchers in the front row swam before his eyes.

Jasmine, solemn, Filli and Kree on her shoulder. Ailsa, paws clasped to her mouth. Nanion, chief of D'Or, eager. Doom, watchful. Dain, pale and intent.

Lief placed his hand upon the golden topaz. For you, Barda, he thought. For Mother and Father, and all at home. "Lief, of Del," he said clearly.

He looked down. The Belt was almost hidden by the hands that touched it. Seven hands of every color, every shape, pressed together in one purpose.

Zeean was speaking again, saying the words that had been agreed.

"Together we, representatives of the seven tribes, renew our ancient vow to unite under the power of the Belt of Deltora, and swear loyalty to Adin's rightful heir."

"We swear," the seven said as one.

And Lief felt the Belt warm under his hand. A thrill ran through him. The topaz was gleaming golden through his fingers. His mind sharpened. The Belt grew hotter, hotter until he was forced, like his companions, to draw his hand away. But by that time, he knew.

The heir was here, in this room.

He looked up. His gaze swept over the people in front of him. Fixed on one. One whose body was trembling, but whose face was shimmering with light as he stepped forward.

Dain.

How could I not have seen? Lief thought, staring in wonder as gasps of shock sighed through the crowd. How could I not have guessed?

Dain, whose very name was a clue, an anagram, made up as it was from the letters that also formed the name "Adin." Dain, who had grown up on an isolated farm, not far from where they now stood. Who had learned the ancient royal art of archery, and as much as his parents could teach him of Deltora's history. Dain — who was quiet, obedient, and dutiful like his father, dark and delicate like his Toran mother. The name he had given his mother — Rhans

— was only Sharn in another form. Yet no one had seen it.

How well he had kept his great secret! Only once had he come close to revealing it. When he had lain by the cracked stone in Tora's heart, stunned and broken by shock and despair.

The tension in the room seemed to crackle as Lief picked up the Belt and moved slowly forward.

Dain waited. The trembling had stopped. He was holding his head high, now. A quiet dignity seemed to have settled over his shoulders like a fine cloak. The smooth skin of his face and hands glowed with light.

My father served and protected his father, thought Lief. Now I will serve and protect him.

He stretched out his hands. The Belt hung loosely between his fingers, for the first time catching the light. He felt a strange reluctance to let it go. He glanced at Jasmine. She nodded, her eyes shining.

This is what we have striven for, Lief thought. This is what was meant to be. He stared at the Belt, taking one last look at the stones that gleamed in the steel medallions. So hard-won, so beautiful . . .

Then he blinked. The ruby was not red, but palest pink. The emerald was dull as a stone. The amethyst had paled to soft mauve. The blood rushed to Lief's head, and his heart begin to pound.

"Danger! Evil!" he gasped. "Here — "

A bloodcurdling shriek split the air. Something

huge burst, slavering, through the door. Then, with a sound like thunder, a blast of wind tore through the room, blowing out the candles, throwing Lief backwards into darkness. He scrambled blindly on the hard floor, clutching the Belt, crying out for Jasmine, for Dain. The wind beat in his face. He could hear crashing and thudding as people fell and furniture flew, splintering against the walls.

"Lief! The Belt!" he heard Dain screaming. "To me! Oh, quickly — "

His cry was drowned out by the wind, by screaming, by something roaring with savage fury.

Lief staggered to his feet and began battling through the howling darkness in the direction from which the voice had come. Something flew through the air and hit him in the chest with tremendous force, hurling him back against Barda's bed. He slumped over it, gasping for breath, struggling to rise.

Then there was a tremendous, rumbling crash from the doorway and the wind stopped, as suddenly as it had begun.

A ghastly silence fell, broken only by the moans and sobs of injured people. His head spinning, Lief pushed himself away from the bed. As he did so, Barda stirred.

"Cold . . ." Barda whispered. Lief realized that his fall had dragged the blankets from the bed. Feverishly feeling around in the dark, he found them and did his best to spread them over Barda once more.

Then, wincing at the pain in his chest, he managed to stand. "Dain!" he heard Doom shouting. "Dain! Answer me!"

But there was no reply.

Someone lit a torch, using the coals of the fire. Glock. Lief caught a glimpse of his brutish face, weirdly lit by flickering light. Glock had a great bruise on his forehead. One of his eyes was swelling and darkening. But still he held the torch high, sweeping it from side to side so that great shadows leaped around the walls.

Lief saw Ailsa, curled on the floor like a great stone; Gla-Thon, staggering from among the remains of the table that had held the belt; Doom, his face smeared with blood; Zeean clutching Manus for support; Jasmine murmuring to Filli. The door was torn from its hinges. The opening was blocked by a mass of collapsed wood and rubble . . .

And Dain was gone. His dagger was lying on the floor where he had dropped it. Dazed, Lief walked over to it. Then he bent and picked it up. The tip of the blade was stained with blood. Dain had tried to fight his attacker. But he had stood no chance.

Sliding the dagger into his belt, Lief thought of the moment he had hesitated before handing over the Belt of Deltora. Perhaps if he had not given in to that feeling of reluctance — if he had passed the Belt to Dain at once — none of this would have happened. Dain would have been safe. They would all have been safe.

Sick with pain and guilt, he looked down at his hands, and his stomach lurched as he realized he was no longer holding the Belt. He looked around wildly, then realized that, of course, he must have dropped it on Barda's chest when he fell against the bed. It was safe there, covered in blankets. He would get it in a moment. When his head had stopped spinning. When he could breathe properly again. When this sickness passed.

He slid to the ground and crouched there, like a wounded animal.

"Dain has been taken!" Fardeep was whispering.

"It was a creature of darkness that did the deed," snarled Glock. "I saw it, as it burst in. A wolf — huge — with a yellow mouth. Then, it changed to a fiend. Even larger. And slimy red, like blood!"

A terrible thought came to Lief's mind. He wet his lips, afraid to put it into words.

Glock's eyes narrowed. He pointed a stubby finger at Lief. "You know something!" he growled. "I see it in your face. What was this thing?"

The words caught in Lief's throat as he spoke. "It sounds — like . . ."

"Like the last and most wicked of all the sorceress Thaegan's children," Doom finished for him. "The only one of that foul brood that still prowls the northeast. Ichabod."

"We have been betrayed," hissed Gla-Thon.

Glock bared his teeth and glared around the

room. His eyes fixed on Manus. "You came from the northeast, Ralad man," he snarled, clenching his fists. "You led the monster here! Admit it!"

Quaking, too shocked and afraid to speak, Manus shook his head. Nanion of D'Or moved to stand beside him. "If we were followed, we were unaware of it," he said sternly. "Keep your insults to yourself, Jalis."

"Do . . . not . . . fight." The words were soft, mumbled. But they broke the angry silence like a shout. For it was Barda who had spoken — Barda, struggling to sit up, to look around him. Jasmine shrieked piercingly and flew to his side, her hair wildly tangled, her small face pale in the glow of the lantern she had coaxed to life.

"Fighting . . . will profit us nothing!" Barda said, his voice growing stronger.

"It is a miracle!" Zeean breathed, staring.

It is the Belt, Lief thought. The Belt. It must be.

But already Doom was striding towards the door. "We must dig our way out of this place and give chase," he snapped. "Every moment we delay means that Dain is closer to death!"

"He is dead already," Glock growled. "The monster will by now have torn him limb from limb."

Doom's head jerked up, as though he had just remembered something. "Where is Steven?" he asked sharply.

In the silence that followed, they heard a faint

sound. A scratching sound, coming from the rubble that blocked the doorway.

"Steven!" Doom shouted.

"Yes!" a voice answered weakly. "I am here. Trapped. The building collapsed upon us as we tried to give chase. Even Nevets could not free us. Doom — it was Ichabod. Ichabod has Dain!"

"We thought as much," said Doom grimly.

"I could see nothing, but I could hear him laughing as he ran away," the faint voice called. "Laughing at Dain. He was saying — that if Dain was king, it was only right that he take him to where the king belonged. To Del."

10 – The Road to Del

Had Ichabod been under orders to capture the heir? Or had it been his own idea to snatch Dain? There was no way of knowing. But of one thing Lief could be sure. He and his companions had done exactly what they had sworn not to do. They had led the Shadow Lord to the heir.

And another thing is certain, Lief thought, as he and the others dug their way out of the shelter that had become their prison. If Dain is being taken to Del, we must follow — alone, if necessary.

But there was no doubt in anyone's mind. The seven tribes would remain united. At dawn, a party left for Del, Ailsa farewelling them tearfully. Doom had made his plans without delay.

"We will travel in small groups, far enough away from one another not to be seen," he said. "This is our best chance of reaching Del unnoticed."

"We will not reach it unnoticed if there is a spy within our ranks," muttered Gla-Thon.

Doom's face hardened. "No one is to be left alone for an instant, except for Steven, who will drive the caravan," he snapped. "Does anyone wish to question Steven's loyalty?"

Not surprisingly, no one dared do that.

The caravan went first, with Barda hidden inside. He was still weak, but he had refused to be left behind. On the right flank moved Manus and Nanion. On the left flank were Gla-Thon and Fardeep. Bringing up the rear were Doom, Zeean, and Glock. And in the center walked Lief and Jasmine, with Filli and Kree.

Lief still carried Dain's dagger. It had been precious to Dain. It would be returned to him — that, Lief had sworn. The point of its blade was deeply stained. No matter what Lief did, it would not come clean.

In the distance, Del-io,
Del-io, Del-io!
Two hours' rest, then on we go,
To Del-i, el-io!

Steven's voice sounded as jolly as if he really was just a simple pedlar. But his message was clear. He could see the outskirts of Del. He was stopping to rest.

"Why must we stop?" Jasmine muttered crossly.

Lief glanced at her. "Because it was agreed we would," he murmured. "Because we want to arrive in Del after dark. And we are tired. You sleep first."

They had been moving by the road's edge, where thick bushes gave plenty of cover. Lief watched as Jasmine settled herself for rest. He knew she would be asleep in moments. That was her way, no matter how uncomfortable the place, or how dangerous the time.

He sat with his back to a tree and touched the Belt, once again fastened around his waist. The Belt had halted Barda's slow drift towards death. But how? Surely none of the gems had the power to cure weakness due to blood loss. Perhaps the diamond . . .

Quietly, he drew out *The Belt of Deltora* and found the section on the powers of the diamond.

† **Diamonds . . . give courage and strength, protect from pestilence, and help the cause of true love.**

Still Lief was unsatisfied. Restlessly, he skimmed the pages, glancing at phrases here and there. A few he had forgotten. Most were very familiar to him.

† **The amethyst . . . calms and soothes. It changes color in the presence of illness, loses color near poisoned food or drink . . .**

† **The topaz protects its wearer from the terrors of the night. It has the power to open doors into the spirit world. It strengthens and clears the mind . . .**

✝ **The emerald . . . dulls in the presence of evil, and when a vow is broken. It is a remedy for sores and ulcers, and an antidote to poison.**

✝ **The great ruby . . . grows pale in the presence of evil, or when misfortune threatens its wearer. It wards off evil spirits, and is an antidote to snake venom.**

✝ **The opal . . . has the power to give glimpses of the future, and to aid those with weak sight . . . The opal has a special relationship with the lapis lazuli, the heavenly stone, a powerful talisman.**

Suddenly impatient, Lief snapped the book closed. Jasmine stirred, then abruptly her eyes opened.

"I am sorry —" Lief began. But she shook her head.

"Something is coming," she hissed, sitting up. "A horse-drawn wagon. Travelling away from Del."

Soon Lief himself could hear the sound of plodding hooves and rumbling wheels. He peered through the bushes and, to his amazement, saw Steven's caravan trundling towards them. There was no jingling sound, for the bells had been taken from the horse's reins.

Steven was singing, but very, very softly. No one but people very near the road could have heard him. As he came closer, Lief could hear that he was crooning the same verse over and over again.

Come out, Twig and Birdie-o!
Little creatures lying low?
Others rest, but we must go,
Twig and Birdie-o!

"It could be a trap," Jasmine breathed. "He could be Ol."

"I do not think so," Lief whispered back. "He is calling us by the false names we used in Rithmere. Barda must have given them to him."

"Glock knows them also!" Jasmine hissed. But already Lief was crawling out from the bushes. She sighed and clambered after him.

Steven saw them, smiled broadly, and stopped the caravan. "So there you are," he said in a low voice, climbing down. "Into the back with Barda, quickly."

"But this is not the plan!" Lief objected. "We are to meet with the others in the grove of trees outside the Del wall, just after dark. If we go with you now, we will arrive before sunset, and alone."

"Indeed," Steve nodded. "Barda will explain all to you. He and I have been talking. I opened a fresh jar of honey for him before we began our journey, and it seems to have done him good. See here!"

He flung the caravan doors wide. And there was Barda, sitting up and grinning.

"Barda! You are well!" Jasmine exclaimed.

Barda shrugged. "Not completely. I would not

relish a fight with an Ol." His grin broadened. "But I could certainly give a small pirate something to think about. Now, get in, quickly. We must be off."

"Why?" demanded Lief, as he and Jasmine reluctantly obeyed.

"If we reach Del before sunset, Steven can drive straight in. He will look like any pedlar hurrying to reach home before the laws against being on the streets at night come into force," Barda explained rapidly. "The gates are always crowded at that hour. The Guards will not bother to search the caravan. And standing with the other carts in the yard beside the market square, it will not be noticed. When it is dark, we can slip away."

"But why change the plan?" Lief was confused.

A rueful expression crossed Barda's face. "First, because the important thing is to get the Belt to Dain, wherever he may be imprisoned. The three of us, I believe, can do this better alone. Second —" He broke off.

"Second," said Steven quietly, "we are both certain that there is a spy in our party. That spy may have a secret way of communicating with the Shadow Lord — a way no one would suspect. If so, our plan could already be known in Del. We could be moving into a trap. We cannot risk that. We cannot risk losing the Belt."

"So we decided to go our own way," said Barda. "Without telling another soul."

"Not even Doom?" asked Jasmine, wide-eyed.

Again, Steven and Barda exchanged glances. "No," said Steven soberly, closing the doors. "Not even Doom."

11 - The Square

Another stuffy, jolting hour. Steven's voice, singing softly, telling what he could see. Terrifying, tense minutes as the caravan slowed to join a line of carts passing through the city gates. The shouts of Guards. Then the sudden, achingly familiar sounds of Del. Wheels, bells, people shouting, jostling one another, bumping the sides of the caravan as it rumbled slowly over cluttered, cobbled streets.

And at last . . . stillness. The smell of rotting vegetables. Footsteps moving slowly to the back of the van.

The click of a latch. The doors opening a crack. Steven's face, tense, peering in, the sky a dimming orange glow behind him. Steven climbing into the van, pulling the doors closed behind him and holding them shut.

"All seems quiet," he whispered. "The streets are empty. There are no Guards about."

"Then where are they all?" Jasmine hissed. She put her hands up to Filli, who was whimpering, nuzzling into her collar.

"Del is a big place," Barda growled. "Perhaps they are guarding the walls. Perhaps they are around the palace . . ."

"Or perhaps they are waiting outside the walls, in the grove of trees — for us!" said Steven.

Lief shuddered. That would mean that there was indeed a spy in their ranks. It would mean that their friends were at this moment walking into a trap. He began to speak, but Barda held up his hand.

"If that is so," he said harshly, "we must only be glad that the Belt is safe here. But our friends will not be unprotected. Steven will go now to the meeting place, if he can escape the city."

"I will escape, one way or another," Steven said grimly. "And I will attend the meeting. To explain — or to settle a score." He clasped Barda's hand, then Lief's, then Jasmine's. "Good fortune," he said huskily. "May I see you again, and soon."

Silently, the four companions climbed from the van. Rats gnawing on piles of vegetable scraps shrilled and scattered around their feet. Steven patted the old horse, which was nibbling at a wilted green leaf. "Wait," he murmured. The horse nodded, snuffling softly.

Threading their way through a crowd of battered carts, they stole to the end of the small yard. But before they could enter the market square, there was a sudden commotion. A door was flung open with a crash. Rough voices and heavy boots burst, echoing, into the night. The light of many torches lit the darkness.

Hastily, the companions drew back into the shadows of the yard. The sound grew louder. There were crashes, grunts, the chink of stone. What was happening? Unable to contain his curiosity any longer, Lief peered cautiously around the corner.

Torches were blazing everywhere. Ten Grey Guards were working in the middle of the square. They were heaving huge blocks of stone into place to make a stepped pyramid with a flat top. Through the center of the pyramid rose a tall pole, towering high and held in place by the blocks that surrounded it.

"Where's the freak?" one Guard bawled. "The Ichabod?"

"It's in the palace, feeding," growled another. "It'll be down here presently, for more. It prefers its meat cooked, they say."

There was a gale of harsh laughter. Lief's skin began to crawl.

"Get up to the top, Bak 6!" barked another Guard. "There'll be trouble if we aren't ready when they bring the others." He strode over to the shadows and came back hauling what looked like a bundle of rags.

"They got them, then, Bak 1?" called the first Guard, climbing to the top of the pyramid. He had a length of rope and an oil jar in his hand.

"Easy. Knew exactly where they'd be, and when, didn't they?" Bak 1 was heaving the bundle up the steps towards the pole. "They got the old woman first, so she couldn't try any of her hocus-pocus. After that it wasn't too bad. The big, ugly one took a bit of time. And the gnome gave some trouble, they say. Killed three Quills and a Pern on her own. But they fixed her in the end."

Lief's heart seemed to stop. He heard the sharply drawn breaths of his companions behind him, but did not turn. Rigid with horror he watched as Bak 1 pulled the bundle upright against the pole and Bak 6 began tying it into place.

It was Dain. Dain, silky hair flopping forward, the side of his pale face flickering in and out of view in the light of the torches. As Lief watched, he slowly raised his head. His eyes opened and widened in terror.

There was a heavy, panting sound behind Lief, and a rough movement. "No!" Steven's voice rasped. "Nevets! Not while the Guards are close to Dain. They have daggers, blisters . . . They will kill him at once, if you strike now. Wait, I beg you!"

There was a moment of struggle. Then the panting eased. The movement stopped.

"Awake at last, your majesty?" Bak 1 was sneering. "That's good." He beckoned, and his fellows began toiling up towards him, their arms full of dead branches. As they dumped the wood around Dain's feet, piling it high, Bak 6 sprinkled it with oil.

"This'll keep him nice and warm," he sniggered. Then he looked up, squinting into the torchlight. "The others are coming with the prisoners," he said. "Party can start anytime. Someone had better get Fallow. Bak 3 — you go."

"He won't come," whined Bak 3. "Ever since he heard that story about the three being sighted in the west, he's stopped worrying. He's locked in that room with his green light. You can see it under the door. And you know he — "

"He'll come for this," growled Bak 1. "There'll be trouble if he misses it. Go on!"

As Bak 3 grumbled away, there were shuffling, clinking sounds from the side of the square nearest the city gates. The next moment, a group of stumbling figures came into view. Some were being dragged by Guards, other were walking alone, their legs weighed down with heavy chains.

Lief searched the faces. There was Gla-Thon, her hair sleek, wet with blood, her left arm hanging uselessly by her side. Manus, shivering with fear, came next. Behind him, Fardeep and Nanion supported Zeean, who hung limply between them. And, dragged on his belly behind the last of the Guards, his body thumping over the cobbles, wrists bleeding freely as the straining chains bit deeply into his flesh was . . . Glock.

Only one person was missing.

"So now we know," muttered Barda.

Steven's great body had begun to tremble all over. Lief glanced at him fearfully.

The huge man's eyes were fixed on Dain. They were changing from yellow to brown, brown to yellow. His mouth was twitching, his flesh quivering, as he fought Nevets for control. "When I give the word, Lief must run to the boy," he growled thickly. "You others — guard Lief as best you can. We will do the rest. But keep away from us. Keep away!"

Lief tore his eyes from the terrible, writhing face, looked around again. Only Bak 1 and Bak 6 stood beside Dain, now. But both still had their daggers drawn.

Lief's fingers felt numb as he reached for Dain's dagger. If he managed to reach Dain alive, he would use the dagger to cut the ropes. That would be fitting. That would be . . .

But the dagger had gone. Lief looked down, blinking stupidly. The dagger must have fallen from his belt, unnoticed. Probably when he was climbing into the caravan on the road to Del.

A lump rose in his throat. Somehow this small loss seemed a symbol of his great failure. He had thought of himself as his king's protector. What folly!

He glanced at Jasmine, rigid beside him. Her eyes were narrow and intent. Her lips were firm. Behind her, Barda towered. He had drawn his sword. His face still showed signs of his illness, but his brow was furrowed with determination.

Lief shook himself. This was no time for weakness. He turned back to face the pyramid and drew his own sword. The sword his father had made for him. That, too, could cut ropes. Could free his king. That, too, was fitting.

Bak 1 grinned cruelly as the chained group came to a stop in front of the platform. "You've got a rare treat in store," he snarled. "You're to witness a great event, before you die."

He looked down, annoyed, as Bak 3 hurried into his view. "Where's Fallow?" he snarled.

Bak 3 shook his head. "He wouldn't answer the door!" he panted. "I told you!"

"Then we'll begin without him!" Bak 1 snapped. "And he'll face the consequences when the master comes!" He jerked his head at Bak 6, who sprang down to the ground, snatched up a torch, and held it up to him.

The prisoners struggled vainly in their chains, their faces masks of horror. Dain leaned back against the pole and closed his eyes.

Lief held himself ready. Ready . . .

"Now, traitors," snarled Bak 1, raising the torch.

"Watch your puny king scream for mercy as he burns." He touched the torch to the wood, then jumped to safety as flames began to leap.

"NOW!" The roar echoed around the square. Not just one voice, but two. And both of them like thunder.

12 - Desperation

Lief ran like the wind, dodging every hand that clutched at him, every blister that flew at him. He did not look behind him. He barely heard the screams, the snarling fury, the shouted orders that ended in shrieks of terror. Jasmine and Barda were on either side of him, but they could not keep pace. In seconds he had reached the platform. Alone he leaped up to the top, sliced through the ropes that bound Dain, pulled the limp body from the flames.

Eyes streaming in the smoke, he swung the boy further down the platform and let him go. Dain staggered, then stood, swaying, on his own feet. Lief grappled with the clasp of the Belt of Deltora. At last it slid apart. He pulled the Belt from his waist . . .

There was a mighty crash, a bellowing roar. Lief spun around. Jasmine and Barda stood teetering on the edge of a gaping hole that had opened in the square. Flaming torches were scattered around them. Nevets, Steven, and a host of Guards had disappeared. The Guards' screams echoed hideously up into the night for a single moment, then were choked off. The ground shook as Nevets raged against the walls of his prison.

Rats poured from the little yard where the caravan stood. As they ran they shimmered and paled, rising into wavering white flames with coals for eyes and gaping, toothless mouths. And in the core of every one was the Shadow Lord's mark.

Lief whirled back to Dain, the Belt dangling from his hand, his mind blank with horror and confusion. A trap had been set for Nevets. They had been betrayed! Their plans had been known. But how? No one knew of Barda and Steven's scheme. No one . . .

And then he saw the dagger on Dain's belt. Unsheathed, the dagger gleamed in the fire's fierce light. Its tip shone bright silver. Lief looked away from it. Up into Dain's dark, dark eyes. And in those eyes, unveiled at last, he saw the answer to all his questions.

"You," he said quietly.

Dain smiled. "I made an error," he said. "I should have put the dagger aside when I returned to this form. How fortunate you did not notice it before you ran to me. That would have spoiled my plan."

His hand swung, striking Lief's arm a tremendous blow, knocking the Belt into the fire. With a cry, Lief grabbed for it. But Dain had his wrist in a grip of icy steel. Dain's eyes narrowed, and suddenly Lief's sword was white-hot. It fell from his blistered hand and clattered, useless, down the steps of the platform.

"Still, I am glad you know, human," Dain hissed. "I want you to know what a fool you have been. And it does not matter now. For now the Belt of Adin cannot harm me. Soon it will be nothing but melted scrap."

He pointed at the remaining Guards. They were open-mouthed, devastated by what had happened to their companions. "Take the prisoners to the palace!" he shouted shrilly. "They have served their purpose."

"No! Let them go!" Lief cried. "You have the Belt! What more do you want?"

Dain's huge, dead eyes glittered. "When I call him, my master will come," he sneered. "He will see you, and your companions, and all the other traitors I have found and brought together here. Then I will be his favorite, ruling this land for him as the soft, Lumin-soaked failure in the palace never could. And you — you will die in torment amid the ruins and ashes of all you love."

His mouth twisted in scorn at the expressions on Lief's face. "You fool! You never dreamed that Ichabod was acting under my orders. That he had not carried me away, but was running alone in the dark, babbling of Del! And when you found the dagger I had become, you did not suspect it for a moment — even though you knew that Grade 3 Ols could take any shape they wished. You put it in your own belt, as I knew you would, snivelling for my loss, little knowing that you were carrying me with you from that time on. I was watching your every move. Listening to your every plan. Waiting to see how best I could destroy the devil Steven and that accursed Belt. And when I knew enough — I left you, and came here to prepare . . . this."

He waved his hand at the seething square. But Lief held his gaze, and did not look away. Lief had seen a movement behind Dain. Someone crawling up the steps of the platform towards him. A hawklike face. A pale, ragged scar. Tangled black hair. Slowly, slowly . . .

"I trusted you, Dain," said Lief. "I thought you were the heir."

Dain sneered. "As you were supposed to do from the first, human. It was what I was created for. I acted my part perfectly, did I not? I made no mistakes."

"You did," Lief said. "You should not have entered Tora. That was your vanity — and it was nearly your death, was it not?"

For the first time, Dain's eyes flickered, and dread brushed his face. But he did not answer.

Keep him talking. Keep him looking at me.

"And you failed to kill Barda with the poison you fed him, little by little," Lief went on doggedly. "Of course, I should have known why he was weakening. I had forgotten. When the amethyst dims, that is a sign of poisoned food. But you had forgotten something, too. The emerald is an antidote to poison. It cured him."

Dain's lip curled. "When he is facing my master, he will wish it had not," he spat.

Nearer . . .

"You feared Barda," Lief said. "He knew too much about the king, and the palace. You realized he was a danger to your scheme when he saw so easily through the false note left with the skeletons. Another of your precious master's plans that fell in ruins!"

By now Dain was breathing heavily. His twisted face was hardly recognizable as that of the delicate, modest boy Lief had known so long.

"My master had many plans, human," he rasped. "And I was the most deeply hidden one. How often I wished I could inform on you, or kill you while you slept! But that was forbidden. My master had ordered me to peace and silence. I was his final weapon, to be used only if every other plan failed,"

"You contacted him once," said Lief. "You told him our names."

Soon . . .

Dain clawed at his chest in remembered pain. "I was — corrected, for that," he said sullenly. "So then I made my own plans. And now my time has come."

Without warning, he threw his head back.

"Master!" he screamed. "It is time!"

A clap of thunder shook the earth. Great red clouds began to roll across the sky from the north, blotting out the stars. Dain faced Lief, eyes gleaming.

"The armies of the Shadow Lord have risen!" he shrieked. "Those throughout the land who have dared defy him will be destroyed. And *you* have brought his wrath down on all their heads. You and your companions have done it all, Lief of Del!"

Doom!

With a cry, Doom leaped upon Dain, knocking him down, his sword plunging for the heart. But Dain twisted like a snake, his body dissolving, rising again in a column of sickly white. Icy mist coiled around him. He whirled around, his fingers reaching for Doom's throat. Long, thin fingers, bringing with them the chill of death.

Lief staggered back, shuddering in a cold that was beyond imagining. The fire wavered, and went out.

Doom was on his knees. The Ol that had been Dain was laughing, laughing, pressing forward, intent on destruction. Shouts and groans rang from the square as Jasmine and Barda, torches blazing, held back a hundred crawling Ols, and the prisoners were dragged away. The sky was a mass of scarlet cloud.

Sobbing, Lief crawled to the fire. He scrambled among the dying embers, his fingers burning and freezing by turns. He found the Belt, staggered to his feet. The Belt was covered in white ash. But it was whole. The ash dropped from its gleaming length. The gems flashed under the red sky.

Now!

With the last of his strength, Lief threw the Belt around the Ol's waist. With both hands he pulled it tight.

And the Ol screamed, throwing up its arms so that Doom fell heavily down the stone steps. Smoke rose from the place where the Belt gripped, and beneath the smoke the shuddering white flesh began to melt. The Ol twisted, trying to break free. But already it was dying. One face alone loomed from its melting white. The face of Dain, in all his moods: timid, beseeching, tearful, laughing, teasing, dignified, brave . . .

Lief bent, choking, as his stomach heaved. But he held tightly to the Belt, squeezing his eyes shut. And when at last he opened his eyes, there was only an ugly puddle of white dripping down the stone steps.

He clasped the Belt around his waist and threw himself down to the bottom of the pyramid, to where Doom lay. Doom was muttering, shuddering with cold. His lips were blue. Great red marks wound around his neck. There was a swelling bruise on his brow.

"Lief!"

Lief looked up wildly. Jasmine and Barda were racing towards him. The Ols in the square were not coming after them. They were wavering, aimlessly clustering together, as though they were confused. It was as though the source of their power had been struck a blow by the destruction of the great one among them.

But already some of them were starting to recover. And the red clouds were tumbling, boiling, as they raced towards the city.

Frantically hauling Doom to his feet, Lief tried to think. Where could they go? Where could they hide?

Then the answer came to him. Where he had always gone when he was in trouble.

Home.

13 - The Forge

The forge was dark, desolate. The Shadow Lord's brand was on the gate. But there was shelter, heat, water. And, for the moment, there was safety.

They lit a fire and wrapped Doom in blankets. They gave him Queen Bee honey and bathed his wounds. At last he seemed to rouse. His eyelids flickered, opened. He stared blankly at the flames leaping in the fireplace.

"Where . . . ?" he mumbled huskily. He put his hand to his throat, and then to the swelling on his forehead.

"Do not try to speak," Lief whispered. Doom turned his head to look at him. His eyes were confused, without recognition.

"The blow on his head was severe," said Jasmine, pacing the room restlessly. "He needs to re-cover."

"Time is what we do not have." Barda moved to the window and peered cautiously through the curtains. "When they realize we have escaped, they will look here, for certain. We must move very soon."

But Lief was watching Doom. The man was staring around the room, his brow creased in a puzzled frown as his gaze lingered on tables, chairs, cushions. It was as though the place was somehow familiar to him. Then he caught sight of Jasmine. His face lightened. His lips moved.

"Jasmine!" Lief hissed. "Come, quickly."

Jasmine hurried to the fire and crouched beside Doom. He raised a hand and touched her cheek. His lips moved again. The words were faint, so faint they could hardly be heard.

"Jasmine. Little one. You . . . have grown so like her. So like . . . your mother."

Jasmine jerked away from him, shaking off his hand as if it was a spider. "How would you know this? My mother is dead!" she cried angrily.

"Yes. My dear love . . . dead." Doom's face creased with grief. His eyes filled with tears. Lief's heart gave a great leap.

"Jasmine . . ." he whispered.

But Jasmine, half sobbing, had turned away.

Doom's eyes had closed once more. But again he

spoke. "They . . . refuse refuge, dear heart," he mumbled, his fingers curling as though he were crumpling a note in his hand. "We . . . must turn back . . . go east of Del, instead of west . . ."

Lief held his breath, realizing that Doom was reliving a time long forgotten. The blow to his head had unlocked the door in which memory had lain.

"We must," Doom murmured. "The news . . . Guards . . . waiting on the western road. All the women with child — killed. We will go east . . . to the Forests. They will not think of looking for us there." He paused, and seemed to listen. His mouth curved into a tender smile as a beloved voice spoke to him in memory.

Jasmine had turned around. Tears were rolling down her cheeks. Filli made tiny, worried sounds and Kree clucked unhappily. Absently, she put her hand up to her shoulder to soothe them, but her eyes were fixed on Doom.

"Danger?" Doom sighed. "Yes, dear heart. But all is danger now. We will take care. We . . . will survive. Our child will be safe. Grow strong, until it is time . . ."

Lief's heart was hammering in his chest. He could scarcely breathe. He saw that Barda had turned from the window and was staring in wonder.

Doom's head moved restlessly. "Little one . . . Jasmine . . ."

Jasmine put her hand in his. "I am here, Father," she said softly.

Doom tried to open his eyes once more, but his lids were heavy. "Poor, brave little girl child," he murmured. "No playmates but the birds and animals. No playthings but the ones the Forests could provide. No books, no comfort. And fear . . . always fear. So many times we wondered if we had done right. We did not regret our choices for ourselves. But for you . . ." His voice trailed off. He was slipping once more into sleep.

"I was happy, Father," Jasmine brushed angrily at her tears. "I had you and Mamma. I had games, songs, rhymes." She tugged at Doom's sleeve, trying to rouse him. "One rhyme I loved especially, because it had pictures," she babbled. "You gave it to me, Father. Remember?"

Doom made no reply. Desperately she released his hand and began rummaging in the pockets of her jacket. Her treasures spilled upon her lap — feathers and threads, a broken-toothed comb, a scrap of mirror, coins, stones, bark, scraps of paper . . . At last, she found what she was looking for. The oldest paper of all — grubby, and folded many times.

Carefully she unfolded it, and shook it in front of Doom's unconscious face. "I still have it," she cried. "See?"

Scarcely able to believe what he was seeing, Lief looked up to meet Barda's eyes. Endon's childhood rhyme. The rhyme that told of the secret way into the palace. Repeated in this very room by Lief's father when the story of Endon and Sharn's escape was told. Here was the one proof that could not be denied. And Jasmine had been carrying it, all along.

His mind flew back to that moment at Withick Mire, when the seven tribes had sworn on the Belt. He had known then, *known*, that the heir was present.

And he had been right.

With shaking fingers he took the Belt of Deltora from his waist. He touched Jasmine's arm. She turned to him, her face anguished. He held out the Belt.

Her eyes widened in shock as she understood him. She shrank away, shaking her head.

"Jasmine, put it on!" Barda thundered. "Doom is Endon. You are his daughter. You are the heir to Deltora!"

"No!" Jasmine cried. She shook her head again, scrambling away from Lief as Kree screeched, fluttering on her shoulder. "No! It cannot be! I do not want it! I cannot do it!"

"You can!" Lief urged. "You must!"

She stared at him defiantly for a single moment. Then, her face seemed to crumple. She crawled to her feet and stood waiting. Lief went to her and, holding his breath, looped the Belt around her slim waist, fastened it . . .

And nothing happened. The Belt did not flash, or shine. Nothing changed. With a great, shuddering sigh Jasmine pulled at the clasp and the Belt dropped to the floor at her feet.

"Take it back, Lief," she said dully. "I knew it was wrong."

"But — but it cannot be wrong!" Lief stammered. "You are the heir!"

"And if I am," Jasmine said, still in that same, dead voice, "then all we have been told about the Belt is false. Doom — my father — has been right all along. We have pinned our lives, and our hopes, on a myth. An old tale made for people who wanted to believe in magic."

Barda slumped into a chair and buried his face in his hands.

Lief stooped and picked up the Belt from the floor. As he fastened it about his waist once more, he felt numb. Why had the Belt not shone? Was it because Jasmine was unwilling?

Or — was the Belt itself at fault? Could one of the gems be false? No. The Belt had warmed to each of the gems in turn. It had sensed them. It knew them.

He moved away from the fire, away from the silent Barda, and Jasmine kneeling beside the sleeping Doom. He wandered out of the room, into the darkness beyond. Then he felt his way to his own small room, and lay down on the bed, hearing its familiar creak.

The last time he had woken in this room, it had been his sixteenth birthday. The boy who had lain here then seemed a stranger . . .

He leaped up, shocked, as there was a crash and a shout from the front of the house.

"I have him!" bawled a rough voice. "Now, the girl! The girl!"

Lief stumbled blindly towards the bedroom door, drawing his sword, hearing with horror the sound of smashing glass, cursing, the thumping of heavy boots. Kree was screeching wildly.

"Mind the bird!" roared another voice. "Ah — you devil!"

Desperately, Lief hugged the wall, feeling his way towards the sound.

"Keep away!" shrieked Jasmine. "Keep away! There are only three of us here, and there are ten of you! Ten!"

Lief froze. Jasmine was warning him that it would be useless to try to interfere. Warning him to keep away, and at the same time making the Guards think that only she, Doom, and Barda were in the house.

He heard a grunt of pain, then the sound of a sharp slap. "That'll teach you to bite!" a Guard snarled. "Three of you, yes! Just where Fallow said you'd be. And one of you out cold. Easy pickings!"

There was a shout of laughter, and the sound of bodies being dragged across the floor. Then . . . there was silence.

Lief waited a few moments, then crept to the living room. The fire still crackled brightly. Warm light flickered over a scene of ruin. Furniture had been thrown everywhere in the struggle. Both windows had been smashed.

Kree hunched on an overturned chair. As Lief approached him, he turned his head and squawked hopelessly.

Lief gripped the hilt of his sword till his knuckles turned white. Suddenly, he was full of a cold anger. "I could not save them, either, Kree," he said. "But it does not end here."

He held out his arm, and Kree fluttered to him. At almost the same moment, through the broken windows came the sound of loud, clanging bells. Lief's stomach churned. He knew what that meant. He had heard the bells before.

"The people are being summoned to the palace, Kree," he said grimly. "And we must go there, too. But not to stand outside the walls with the rest. We must get inside."

He walked to the fireplace and picked up the worn scrap of paper that Jasmine had dropped on the rug. Carefully he refolded it and put it in his pocket.

It was time for the bear to be woken once more.

14 - The Place of Punishment

The chapel was cold and empty as Lief crawled from the secret tunnel and slid the marble tile that had concealed it back into place. Shivering, he pushed open the chapel door and climbed the dark steps beyond, with Kree perched firmly on his arm.

Lief had no plan. No plan at all. But somehow it seemed right that he was here. Where this story began, so it will end, he thought. One way or another.

He peered from the darkness of the steps into the huge space beyond. The ground floor of the palace seemed deserted. But echoing down the vast stairway which wound up to the top floors was a distant, murmuring sound. The sound of a huge crowd.

Lief knew where the sound was coming from. It was floating through the huge open windows of the great hall on the first floor. The people of Del were thronging the hill beyond the palace garden. They were looking up at the Place of Punishment. This was a wooden platform supported on great poles, stretching all the way from the windows of the great hall to the wall that ringed the palace garden. The flag of the Shadowlands, a red hand on a grey background, hung from a flagpole directly above it.

The Place had been built when the Shadow Lord came. The sight of it, even from a distance, had chilled Lief from babyhood. For even tiny children were forced to witness the executions that took place there, and forbidden to turn their heads away. The Shadow Lord wanted all in Del to know the price of rebellion.

And so they did. Once or twice a year they saw terrible sights at the Place of Punishment, and in between those times it remained a constant reminder. The ground below it was heaped with bones. The wall was spiked with skulls. And the edge of the platform itself was hung with a thick fringe of dangling, rotting bodies, each branded with the Shadow Lord's mark.

"People of Del! Behold these traitors!" Lief gripped his sword as the thin, penetrating voice echoed faintly down the stairway. Fallow himself was standing on the Place, addressing the crowd. Usually, one of the Grey Guards conducted the executions. But this, of course, was a special occasion.

Running the secret way, Lief had reached the palace very quickly. Toiling the long way, up the hill, the Guards who had raided the forge could not yet have arrived. But Fallow had six other examples to show the crowd while he waited for news of the capture of those he wanted the most.

Rapidly, Lief looked around him. He knew that there was no chance of reaching the Place from inside the palace. Guards and palace servants always clustered in the windows that edged the platform.

But from what his father had told him, he knew that the kitchens were near. And they would be empty, for all the servants would be upstairs. He could run through the kitchens, outside, and around to where the Place towered. He could climb one of the poles that supported the stage from below.

But — the Place was always well lit. The Guards who stood at the platform's edge would see him the moment his head appeared. They would all have blisters ready in their slings, too, and plentiful supplies in boxes behind them. It was their task to hurl blisters into the crowd at any sign of disobedience.

"If only I could fly like you, Kree," he muttered, glancing at the bird perched rigidly on his arm. "Then I could surprise them from above."

Kree blinked, and cocked his head. Then Lief saw what he must do.

✳

In moments he was in the open air. The dark red clouds hung heavily overhead, casting an eerie glow over the earth. He could hear Fallow's voice clearly.

". . . joined in a plot to overthrow our great

leader. A plot doomed to failure, as all such evil is doomed."

Lief shut the sound from his mind.

Hurry!

The palace loomed above him. Dark, but with plenty of windows, ornaments, and other footholds.

He began to climb. Up, up, past the first floor windows, then up again to the narrow ledge that ran under the windows on the second floor.

The servants who cleaned the windows sat on the ledge often, no doubt. But Lief was standing, and his stomach knotted as he carefully turned until his back was to the wall. Then he began to move, edging along to the corner of the building, around to the side . . .

And below, far to his left, the Place of Punishment stood in a blaze of light.

He edged close. Closer . . .

The Place was thick with Guards. Torches flamed, lighting the darkness. Large red cones stood on each end of the platform. Lief had never seen their like before, and could not imagine their purpose. To one side was a huge metal pot of burning coals. Lief gritted his teeth. He knew *its* purpose only too well.

Fallow was in the center of the stage, holding two chains that were fastened to the necks of a pair of prisoners sprawled at his feet. Six more chained figures stood in a ragged line behind him. Glock.

Zeean. Manus. Nanion. Gla-Thon. Fardeep. All were wounded. Zeean was swaying. Glock could barely stand. Fallow stabbed at them with a bony finger.

"See them, people of Del?" he shrieked. "See these strangers? See their ugly bodies? Their twisted, evil faces? Monsters! Invaders of Del! Double branding, and death!"

A sickening wave of dizziness seized Lief. He pressed his back against the wall, panting. His throat had tightened so that he could hardly breath.

Six Guards strode forward and plunged iron branding rods into the pot of coals. They laughed and spat on the heating metal. Their turn for amusement had arrived.

The Guards facing the crowd raised their slings threateningly.

"Double branding and death!" chanted the people.

Lief gazed desperately over the sea of upturned, shouting faces. He saw no grins of glee or scowls of anger. The faces were absolutely blank — the faces of people beyond hope, beyond despair.

Suddenly, Fallow glanced behind him, at the windows of the great hall. Guards were moving there, stumbling out of the way of another Guard hurrying through. The newcomer signalled to Fallow, nodding excitedly, pointing behind him. Fallow's face changed. A triumphant smile spread over his face and he glanced upward. Lief caught his breath and flattened himself even further against the wall.

But Fallow did not see him. He was looking much higher — to the tower. Seven huge birds perched on the tower roof, their cruel, curved beaks outlined against the scarlet sky. Inside, where once the Belt of Deltora had lain in its glass case, red smoke swirled. And a shadowy figure stood motionless. Watching. Waiting . . .

Lief sidled further along the ledge. Now he was exactly where he wanted to be — on a small stone platform directly above the Place of Punishment, and beside the metal pole that bore the flag of the Shadowlands. Forcing his shaking hands to do his bidding, he pulled his coil of rope from his belt and tied one end of it to the flagpole. He tugged it gently, and knew it would hold.

Fallow swung back to face the crowd. He gestured, and the Guards pulled the six condemned prisoners roughly back, to stand against the palace wall.

"Their punishment can wait!" Fallow cried, his voice cracking with glee. "I can now announce, that, by my orders, our three greatest enemies have been captured! I knew it would be so!"

His face dark with spite and anger, he bent to heave up the crumpled figures at his feet.

And Lief's breath caught in his throat as he saw that the helpless couple were his mother and father.

Ragged, gaunt, they sagged in Fallow's cruel hands.

He shook them by their iron collars, as a dog shakes a rat, then set them back on their feet. They stood, swaying. "These two wretches will see their son before they die!" he snarled. "Behold them! The father and mother of treachery! Now they will pay for the evil they have caused, the lies they have told!"

There was a terrible roaring in Lief's ears. He saw the crowd staring at the prisoners. He saw many of the blank faces crease with pain as they recognized the kind, quiet man and the sweet, lively woman from the blacksmith's forge. Some, perhaps, did not even know their names. But they knew their natures. And so they grieved, hopelessly, for what was to come.

And Lief — Lief slowly unclasped the Belt of Deltora and put it down at his feet. It would have helped him in the fight ahead, but he knew that this was a fight that in the end he could not win. If he was to die, he would not die wearing the Belt. He would not allow it to be part of his defeat and pain. Or let his parents see it trodden into the dust.

He stared down at the precious, mysterious thing that had brought them all to this. It was complete. And it was powerful. Powerful enough to kill Dain. Powerful enough to feel the presence of the heir. And yet . . . somehow it was not perfect. Somehow, they had not discovered its final secret. He was tormented by the feeling that the answer was before his eyes, if only he could see it.

The gems lay gleaming in their steel medallions. The topaz. The ruby. The opal. The lapis lazuli. The emerald. The amethyst. The diamond.

Lief remembered the winning of every one — what he had felt as each stone was added to the chain in turn.

Added . . . in turn . . .

His scalp began to prickle. Well-remembered words from *The Belt of Deltora* swam into his mind:

✝ **Each gem has its own magic, but together the seven make a spell that is far more powerful than the sum of its parts. Only the Belt of Deltora, complete as it was first fashioned by Adin and worn by Adin's true heir, has the power to defeat the Enemy.**

. . . complete as it was first fashioned by Adin . . .

. . . together the seven make a spell . . . a spell . . .

SPELL!

Lief pulled out his dagger, crouched over the Belt. His fingertips tingled as quickly, quickly, he used the dagger's tip to lever the gems from their places, one by one. It seemed to him that they came easily, helping him. Helping him again as he replaced them — but this time in a different order. The right order.

Diamond. Emerald. Lapis lazuli. Topaz. Opal. Ruby. Amethyst.

DELTORA.

With a great sigh, Lief stood up, the Belt of Deltora gleaming in his hands. His breathing had slowed. His hands were steady. He knew, beyond doubt, that at last the Belt was as it should be. Now it was as it had been when first fashioned by Adin, who had used the first letters of the seven tribes' talismans to form the name of their united land. Now it was ready to be claimed by Adin's true heir.

And Jasmine was coming. At any moment she would be dragged onto the platform. Now Lief knew why he had been led to this place. Now he had a plan.

15 - Fight to the Death

There was a sudden confusion of noise from the windows below him. The newest captives were coming through. Fallow shrieked an order. Guards touched torches to the red cones. The crowd gasped in shock as blinding white light hissed and flared. Light flooded the Place, lighting the faces of the prisoners, banishing every shadow, illuminating the whole of the side of the palace almost to the roof.

Bathing Lief in brilliance.

He shrank back, but there was nowhere to hide. And the people of Del, looking up, could see him. See him clearly. His stomach heaved as he waited for them to call out, pointing and exclaiming. Waited for Fallow to turn, for Fallow's eyes to follow the pointing fingers, to sight him, to shriek to the Guards . . .

But there was utter stillness. Utter silence. Lief saw a wide-eyed little child in her mother's arms began to lift a hand. But the mother quickly pushed the hand down, murmuring softly, and the child stilled.

Lief stared, holding his breath. The people of Del stared back, their faces intent. Many knew him well — his friends, their parents, those who had visited the forge while he worked with his father. Others knew him only by sight — as a nuisance, a wild boy running with his friends through the city. Some did not know him at all.

But they knew he was one of them. They saw what was in his hands. And none of them was going to give him away.

Fallow had noticed nothing. He was watching as Jasmine, Barda, and Doom, blindfolded with hoods and heavily chained, were dragged to his side.

Lief measured the distance to Jasmine with his eyes. He took the rope in his right hand. Grasped the Belt firmly in his left . . .

The people watched. Silent. Wishing him well. He felt their thoughts as clearly as if they had shouted them aloud. Flowing through him. Giving him strength.

"Now!" Fallow cried. "Now I show you three traitors who nearly escaped, because a vain and foolish creature, bloated with pride, thinking to be my rival, put his own secret plans into action while I was — occupied with other important duties."

Grinning, he snatched off Jasmine's hood. Then Barda's. But when he saw Doom, the grin vanished.

He took a step back, his face a mixture of fear and rage.

Wait . . .

Leif saw his father turn, look at Doom. He saw his father's eyes light with mingled joy and pain. Saw him stretch out a trembling hand to his boyhood friend.

And saw Doom staring back, his ravaged face suddenly blazing with consciousness, with memory. Then turning this way and that, looking around him, searching urgently for someone he could not find.

Searching for me.

"You fools!" Fallow hissed savagely to the Guards who had brought the prisoners. "This is not one of the three! Where is the boy? The *boy*?"

The Guards mumbled in confusion and backed away.

Now!

Lief jumped, Kree screeching above his head. He swung outward, then let go of the rope and landed just beyond Jasmine, stumbling, then regaining his feet. He lunged for her, the Belt in his hand. He saw her face, wild-eyed with shock, heard Barda shouting, the crowd roaring, Fallow screaming to the Guards. And from the tower, a cry of rage that pierced his flesh, melted his bones, forced him to his knees.

Lightning cracked the boiling sky, streaking towards him. He threw himself aside, rolling, stunned, as it struck the place where he had been kneeling.

With the shriek of splitting wood, the front of the platform collapsed as though a giant had smashed it with a mighty fist. Its two halves tipped towards one another like giant slides, and the nearest Guards toppled, scrambling, shrieking, into the yawning gap between, white hot coals spilling after them.

Lightning flashed again, and again. Roaring thunder shook the trembling earth. And out of the thunder swooped the seven Ak-Baba, their unearthly, wailing cries chilling the blood.

Lief clung desperately to the tilting boards. The crowd was screaming now, screaming to him . . .

But Fallow — Fallow had him. Fallow's icy hand was on his neck, wrenching him upward. The hated, writhing face was close to his, lips drawn back in a snarl of triumph as Lief struggled to draw his sword.

Then, abruptly, the face jerked backwards, eyes bulging. Lief was hurled backwards once more as the icy hand loosened, flew to the thin throat, and clawed desperately at the strangling chains biting deeply into the flesh.

Did Fallow know who had seized him? Did he know who were behind him now, using the last of their strength to heave him, choking, away from his prey?

The ones he had thought too broken to be a threat. Whose chains he had dropped without a thought.

"Father! Mother! Beware!" Lief screamed, clawing his way up the slope towards them. Fallow was feeling for his dagger. He had found it! Lief lunged forward.

"No, Lief!" his father cried. "The Belt! You — "

His voice was silenced as Fallow struck. He crumpled and fell. Lief's mother caught him, and together they crashed onto the groaning boards. She flung out a hand and clutched the edge of the platform to hold them both, her scream lost in the raging of the wind, the shrieking of the Ak-Baba.

Fallow was dragged down with them, caught by the chains wound around his neck. He pulled himself free, writhing on the tipping boards, struggling for breath, struggling to rise. Then he saw the red cone of light sliding slowly towards him. He grabbed for it, seized its base, then saw his danger.

Too late. Slowly, slowly, the cone tipped. Burning white liquid light poured over him, covering him, sizzling, sizzling as he screamed.

There was a roaring, rushing sound above. Lief looked up. Red smoke was gushing from the tower. Red smoke, thick and edged with grey, heavy with menace. Grey light circled and swirled in its depths. And in its center a huge shape was forming. Hands, reaching. Eyes, hungry for revenge.

Lief spun around. He saw Jasmine and Barda facedown on the other side of the platform, clinging on for dear life as the planks tipped more and more steeply. Above them flapped an Ak-Baba, talons outstretched. Kree was darting at the monster's head, yellow eyes flashing as he pecked again and again. The Ak-Baba was screeching in fury, twisting its neck, trying to rid itself of its attacker.

Lief gritted his teeth. Prepared for the jump of his life. Could he do it? Jump that yawning gap and climb up those steep, slippery boards? With the sword in one hand, the Belt of Deltora clutched in the other?

Once, he would have tried it. Now, he had learned wisdom. Steadying himself, he sheathed his sword. He clasped the Belt around his waist . . .

And — time seemed to stand still.

What . . . ?

A rush of heat swept through Lief's body. There was a strange, crackling sound. Then the Belt seemed to explode with light.

A furious roar shook the palace to its core. Red smoke recoiled, hissing, into the boiling clouds. But the gems of the Belt of Deltora blazed like fire, their rainbow brilliance streaming outward, filling the air, banishing the night, dancing on the faces of the cheering, weeping people. And in the center of the light stood Lief. Lief, the true heir of Deltora, revealed at last.

Shrieking, panic-stricken, the Ak-Baba wheeled away, soared upward to the tower. But the tower was empty. And already the red clouds were rolling back to the Shadowlands, a raging malice growling in their depths. A malice that would not die, but which knew that this battle, at least, it could not win.

Astounded, Lief looked around him. Saw his mother smling, sobbing, cradling his father's head in her lap, and Doom kneeling beside them. Saw Jasmine and Barda, clinging together, their faces wild with joy and relief while Kree screeched above them and Filli danced on Jasmine's shoulder. Looked behind him at the shrieking, cheering Manus, Gla-Thon, Nanion, and Fardeep. Saw Zeean raising her head, her eyes shining. And Glock — Glock! — grinning all over his face.

They are safe, Lief thought, his heart swelling. All will be safe now.

The remaining Guards were tearing blisters by the dozen from the boxes and hurling them into the celebrating crowd. But the people had already learned that water and Boolong sap were not harmful. Soon, the Guards would realize their own danger.

For they had been ruthlessly abandoned. As had the Ols, who, their source of power withdrawn, lay with burst and shrivelled hearts in the market square, where at last Steven was climbing from the pit. As had Ichabod, sprawled like a drained sack of red skin over the gnawed bones of his last meal.

And so it would be now, all over the land. As the radiance of the Belt filled Lief, his eyes seemed to pierce darkness and distance. From Raladin to Rithmere, from Dread Mountain to the Valley of the Lost, from Broad River to Withick Mire, fear was vanishing.

Throughout Deltora people were seeing their enemies falling, the clouds of evil in flight. The people were throwing down their weapons in joy, creeping from hiding, embracing their loved ones, and looking up at the sky. Knowing that suddenly, amazingly, a miracle had occurred. And at last they were free.

Lief knew all this. He knew, he accepted, that he was the heir to Deltora. The Belt had proved it beyond doubt. But how? How could this be?

16 - The Last Secret

Dazed, Lief climbed to his parents' side. As he knelt, embracing his mother and bending to his father, he met Doom's eyes. Doom's mouth twitched into a ghost of his old, mocking smile. Do you not yet understand? the smile seemed to ask.

Lief shook his head. Dimly he heard the crowd cheering still. He felt Jasmine and Barda, freed from their chains, sinking down beside him. But he could not move. He could not speak. He could only stare at Doom, his eyes filled with questions.

"The perfect hiding place," Doom murmured. "Was it not? For whoever would suspect? Whoever would suspect that the man and woman who ran from Del that night nearly seventeen years ago were laying a false trail? That they were not the king and queen at all?"

His eyes warmed as he looked at Lief's parents.

"Who would suspect that the king of Deltora could live as a blacksmith? And a queen, a fine lady of Toran blood, could grow vegetables, and spin common yarn? Yet, what was Adin, but a blacksmith?

Then he turned back to Lief, and raised an eyebrow. "And what should be more fitting than that the heir to Deltora be brought up as a common boy, learning without trying the ways of his world, and its people?"

Then, in wonder, Lief saw it. Saw the plan in all its simplicity. A plan based on sacrifice. Based, also, on the confusion and chaos that Del had become. When neighbor lost sight of neighbor, friend lost touch with friend, and no face was familiar.

Doom's plan . . . Doom, who was not Endon, but Jarred. Jarred who, with his beloved wife, had given his identity, his home, and his life to his friend, for the sake of the land they loved. Jarred, who had fled Del that dark night, with the little rhyme that had led him into the palace still in his pocket. No wonder Jasmine was as she was, with parents such as these!

"You had the idea of decoys once before, then, Doom?" he murmured.

Doom nodded. "So it seems. Though I did not know it, when I sent our Toran friends to the west. It is good to think that they, also, are safe." He glanced behind him, and Lief heard the sound of fighting in the palace.

"The Resistance has arrived," Doom said casually. "They will take care of the last of the Guards. Like Barda and Steven, I thought it wise to make a special plan, known to no one else. There is a certain drain-tunnel in Del, that leads to the palace kitchens . . ."

"I think I know it," Lief muttered. "I found it once. On my birthday . . ."

His mother squeezed his hand.

His mother. Not Anna of the Forge, practical and wise in the ways of herbs and growing things. But Sharn, of Tora. The one who could weave like a miracle. The one whose wit and courage had taught him so much.

Lief looked down at his father, the tender, soft-spoken man whose name, he now knew, was not Jarred, but Endon. How could he have not guessed?

How could his gentle father have done the things Jarred was said to have done? Why would the true Jarred have been so bitter about Endon's foolishness?

The face seemed smoothed, softened. It was very calm. The eyes were warm and peaceful. The mouth curved into a smile. Lief heard Barda's quickly indrawn breath, and felt his own eyes burn with tears.

"Do not weep for me," his father murmured. "I am happy. My life is fulfilled. Here, now, at the moment of my death, I have what I have longed for. The knowledge that the evil caused by my fault has been undone. The knowledge that, with my dear wife, I have raised a son who can lead his people wisely, know their hearts."

"Why did you not tell me, Father?" murmured Lief. "Why did you not tell me who I was?"

"While you did not know, you were safe," his father whispered. "And — you had to learn — to love and know the people, and be one of them. That — I had sworn."

"But . . . Barda?" Lief glanced at the big man kneeling so silently beside him.

His mother shook his head. "Barda did not know the truth. He had seen Jarred and Anna leave. He thought they were the king and queen, for that is what we told him. At the palace he had only ever seen us from a distance, dressed and painted in palace fashion. We never told him the secret. We had sworn to keep the plan between the four of us. And when you went on your quest — why, we thought that as soon as the Belt was complete, there would be no need for explanation. We thought it would shine! We did not know . . ."

"We did not know that the order of the gems was important," Doom finished. "How could we? The book told nothing of that."

"It did," Lief said quietly. "But it told it in riddles."

Endon smiled. "That is fitting," he said. "For all along, Lief, this has been a story where nothing is as it seems. I have always liked such tales. For such tales usually have happy endings. . . . As does this one."

His eye closed. Lief clasped his mother's hand, and bowed his head.

✳

Lief, Jasmine, and Barda stood together, looking out into the dawn.

"I am glad it was you, Lief," Jasmine said. "So glad."

Lief looked at her. Her face was smudged with mud. Her hair was tangled. Her mouth was set in a strong, straight line.

"Why?" he asked.

"I could have offered the people nothing," she said, moving away from him. "How could I be a queen? What am I but a wild girl, quick-tempered and troublesome, more at home in a forest than a walled garden?" She tossed her head. "Besides, I cannot stay here. This city is hideous to me. And the palace — a prison!"

"Prison walls can fall," Lief said softly. "Gardens can become forests. Del can be beautiful once more. And as for what you can offer, Jasmine . . ." For a moment, his voice failed him. This was so important. He had to choose his words carefully. But whatever he said must be the truth. Not the whole truth, perhaps, but at least part of it.

"Well?" Jasmine demanded, her shoulders rigid.

"There is much to do," Lief said simply. "So much to do, Jasmine. All over Deltora. Barda, Doom, and I cannot do it alone. We need your courage and your strength. We need you, exactly as you are."

"Indeed," said Barda gruffly.

Jasmine glanced at them over her shoulder. Filli chattered in her ear. Kree screeched on her arm.

"Then, I suppose I will stay — for a while," she said, after a moment. "For, certainly, you need me. As your father needed my father. To get things done."

Lief smiled, and, for once, did not argue.

He was well satisfied.